someone else's love letter

DEBORAH BLUMENTHAL

DIVERSIONBOOKS

Diversion Books
A Division of Diversion Publishing Corp.
443 Park Avenue South, Suite 1008
New York, New York 10016
www.DiversionBooks.com

This is a work of fiction. Names, characters, places and incidents either are the
product of the author's imagination or are used fictitiously. Any resemblance to
actual persons, living or dead, events or locales is entirely coincidental.

For more information, email info@diversionbooks.com

First Diversion Books edition March 2016.
Print ISBN: 978-1-62681-932-0
eBook ISBN: 978-1-62681-931-3

With special thanks to Cathy Fitzpatrick Cleary
and Helen Perry, stylists extraordinaire,
for sharing their stories.

"Women dress alike all over the world:
they dress to be annoying to other women."

—Elsa Schiaparelli

chapter one

There are things you never expect to find in a taxi. Things like love letters. This one was easy to miss, wedged under the driver's seat except for a tiny triangle of icy blue playing peekaboo. I would never have seen it if a stretch limo to our right hadn't turned with no warning, nearly shearing off the front fender.

When the driver slammed the brakes, I was on my way home after three hours inside a walk-in closet. My handbag pirouetted over the seat, releasing a sea of bracelets, beads, scarves, shoulder pads, Miracle Bras, panty hose, scissors, Scotch tape, safety pins, Velcro, Motrin, tampons, and Red Bull. To the barrage of expletives from the driver, I tossed it all together like a crazy salad and stuffed it back into my bag.

That's when I spotted the envelope.

I tugged at the corner and it slid free. The paper was thick, luxurious, and addressed in amethyst ink. I lifted the flap, tracing my finger over the midnight-blue lining embedded with whispery white threads. I held it to my nose.

A faint perfume. Two sheets were neatly folded inside.

Dear Caroline…

I was just a block from home, so I slid it into a jacket pocket and searched for my wallet. After greeting the doorman, I picked up my mail and rushed upstairs to feed Harry, the man of the house, my yellow lab. It wasn't until a week later, when I wore the jacket again, that I thought of the letter.

When important things happen, your mind has a way of fixing the moments into your memory. You recall exactly where you were and why, who you were with, the time of day, even the light. I began reading the letter on the bus up Madison Avenue, passing Calvin Klein, Donna Karan, Barneys, Yves St. Laurent, and Ralph Lauren's flagship store in the Rhinelander Mansion. Only then I didn't try to glimpse the clothes as the shop windows fast-forwarded like frames from a high-fashion video.

It was a crisp fall day, a time of beginnings. For no particular reason, everything felt right in my world when I woke that morning. It was Saturday. The Chinese finger trap of time was looser. My plan was to spend the morning at the Metropolitan Museum of Art and then walk part of the way back through Central Park.

I was in navy D&G flannel slacks, a white ribbed Tory Burch sweater, and Fratelli Rosetti loafers. My jacket was over my arm. On the way to the bus I stopped at Starbucks and asked for Panama La Florentina, the coffee of the day, because the barista behind the counter told me it was similar to their house blend, and anyway, I just liked the way it sounded. Before I left, I put the coffee down and slipped on my jacket.

The only free seat on the bus was the hot seat in the back, always the last to be taken because it was over some motor part that turned it into a radiator. I sat anyway, afraid that if the bus stopped short I'd be faced with litigation. Before I opened the newspaper, I slid my Metrocard into my pocket. That's when I remembered the letter.

I opened the envelope and recalled how much I had admired the stationery, particularly the way the sender put the return address not in the usual places—on the upper left-hand corner or on the flap—but vertically up the left side of the front edge of the envelope, in carefully printed block letters.

> *Dear Caroline, I know you're used to reading emails, not letters. I know you make split-second decisions, and think life's more black and white than gray, but I have to explain…and I beg you to listen.*

He talked about his empty life before they met—the unhappy relationships, his despair at not being able to find the right woman, his feelings of isolation. Then they met and everything changed.

> *How can I explain the way I feel about you?*
> *Let me tell you about a book of letters I read by the physicist and Nobel laureate Richard P. Feynman. His first wife had moved to Albuquerque to be near him when he worked on the Manhattan Project in Los Alamos. She later died there in a sanitarium, from tuberculosis. A year and a half after her death he wrote, "I find it hard to understand in my mind what it means to love you after you are dead. But I still want to comfort and take care of you—and I want*

you to love me and care for me." He ventures that maybe they could still make plans together, but no, he had lost his "idea-woman, the general instigator of all our wild adventures."

"You can give me nothing now yet I love you so that you stand in my way of loving anyone else," he wrote. "But I want to stand there. You, dead, are so much better than anyone else alive."

Before you nothing in my life had real meaning. You're gone now, yet all I think about is you. I live in the shadow of our relationship, pretending you're still with me. Even without you, the memories of our life together mean more than the reality of being with someone else.

Caroline, please, let me see you. At least let me talk to you. Life without you is unthinkable.

A heartfelt plea to win a woman back. It was almost Shakespearean. Only the address wasn't Stratford-upon-Avon, it was downtown Manhattan. I slipped it back into the envelope.

Whose life had I stumbled on? Where did he live, what did he do? Men called, emailed, or sent text messages—they didn't write letters, and if they did, never on handmade paper with deckle edges, a throwback to the fifteenth century.

The writer had style. He was smooth, articulate. The wrappings of his thoughts were as affecting as his words. Just thinking about him set my mind reeling with the possibilities. Where did that leave me?

Captive.

Which made no sense. I was a peeping tom, peering into someone else's emotional life. Still, he was a kindred spirit. He knew the importance of putting things in the proper wrapping too. So never mind Caroline who had tossed away the letter like a losing lottery ticket; maybe he'd like to meet a woman of the cloth who judged letters by their covers.

I gazed out the bus window, forgetting my plans for the day. When I remembered to check the street signs, the bus had passed the Met and was approaching 96th Street. I got off, turned around, and walked the three miles back to Murray Hill, as if it made perfect sense to ride all the way uptown and then go directly back home without stopping anywhere at all in between.

chapter two

A woman with a name that regularly appeared under photos of society events called me to do a closet assessment. I usually shied away from taking on clients outside the city, but something about her commanding voice and her address at the shore intrigued me. In the fall it was an easy two-and-a-half-hour trip to the Hamptons.

Neil Young singing "Heart of Gold" made the claustrophobic drive through the Midtown tunnel bearable. Then onto the sluggish Long Island *Expressway*. No wonder locals call it the L-I-E. Before lunch I was in rural farm country on local roads passing Quogue, all whitewashed and pure, a heavenly haven for city escapees.

Her house was about half an hour further. Southampton homes were palatial, set further apart than in most other communities. The compound overlooked the ocean and the bay on open beachfront with acres of privacy. I followed the circular driveway to the sound of gravel—or maybe diamonds—crunching beneath the tires. I got out and stretched, glancing up to watch the seagulls' ballet. The sea air was misted with salt water and ocean perfume.

The house was a two-story Greek revival flanked by heavy white columns. The doorbell set off a round of barking like gunshots. A woman with honey-colored hair, impeccable posture, and a waspish waist opened the door. Two taut Rhodesian Ridgebacks, each almost half her height, stood on either side of her, sentries staring up at me with shining eyes. All they needed was Santa hats on their heads to make it a perfect Christmas card photo.

"Stay," she commanded.

How could I not dwell on the fact that the breed was intensely prey driven? And there I was, wafting eau d'Harry, who'd sooner lick another animal than eat it.

"I'm Sage Parker," I said, extending my hand.

"Mary Alice Moriarity," she said, taking it. "If the dogs bother you, I'll put them out back."

One of them leaned toward me and sniffed my crotch. I eased back. "They're gorgeous, but it might be better." With the dogs out in the yard, she joined me in the living room, a cavernous space with chairs and couches color-coordinated to the hue of the sand. Out of the corner of my eye, I saw her examining my outfit. I was prepared for that. I never dressed casually. Following a brief exchange about the trip and the weather, we got down to business. "How do we begin?" she said.

"Let's go to your closet so I can get a feel for the kind of clothes you wear."

With a nod, she led the way up a winding mahogany staircase covered with a jewel-toned runner, vibrant despite the patina of Persian history.

"Do you live here year-round?"

"Now I do."

Help a woman with her wardrobe and she'll open her heart to you. As she takes off one outfit and tries another, off comes the protective armor. She'll tell you not only how she feels about her body and sees herself but also how she feels about her life—what she loves and hates, where's she's been, and her hopes for the future. She'll undress herself for you, baring her soul.

Still, it usually took more than the few seconds it takes to climb a flight of stairs to get there. She glanced back at me briefly, head high and defiant.

"My husband moved out," she said, with as much emotion as you'd summon to discuss a chipped nail. Without another word, she strode across the bedroom into a windowless space the size of a guest room. She gestured to an adjacent closet that looked empty. "So I thought now might be the time to start some image work."

It's almost always about more than the clothes. On one level I was a wardrobe consultant, on another a crisis counselor. "The whole business of reassessing a wardrobe is often triggered by some major change," I said, looking through her rack of suits. "I call it an SSE, or shape-shifting experience, meaning both the shape of your body and your life."

A lock of hair sprang free from the short, neat style framing her pale blue eyes and the arched brows that framed them. She smoothed it back. *Handsome* was the word that came to my mind. Midforties, carefully dressed in brown, brown, and brown—her slacks, a shell, a cardigan, the signature Ferragamo flats. Dull, even frumpy. She needed more flair, ease, and style. I wanted to loosen her hair, push up the sleeves of the sweater, give her an armful of bracelets, the right scarf, and low-heeled boots to raise her up. Mary Alice needed contrast, less structure, and for evening, clothes with more drama, maybe satin and fur. I was thinking Ralph Rucci. She could look sexier, more sensual; she had the bones. Right now she was like a carefully set table without the flowers and food.

I walked further into the custom closet with mahogany cabinetry and antiqued brass fittings. Texas-sized, with an island in the middle with narrow drawers for accessories. The Great Santini of closets, organized with military precision, every garment on wide mahogany hangers. Unimaginable to think of an off-center crease here. Not a hemstitch would be loose nor a button missing. Where were the notes detailing when each garment was worn and where?

Brown, black, navy, charcoal, and dark green, like a patchwork of bleakness. No brights, patterns, variation, or sensuality. High-end, but bloodless. No doubt her husband left her for a cheesy blond who dolled herself up in frilly pink chiffon. Someone who loosened his tie and taught him to enjoy Dunkin' Donuts, licking the sweet grease off his fingers.

I started out neutral. "So, how do you feel in color— bright color?"

"Never worn it."

I opened my tote bag and pulled out my cornflower-blue shawl, like a magician pulling a rabbit out of a hat. Whenever I unfolded it, my mother's voice echoed in my head: *If your neck is warm, your whole body is warm.* Health lore said you covered the head to stay warm; still, I suspected she was on to something. "Try this on."

Mary Alice wrapped it around her shoulders and studied herself in the mirror before turning to me. It brought out her eyes and enlivened her complexion.

"You look reborn. The color's perfect."

"How much do you want for it?"

I could have scalped my two-hundred-dollar shawl for ten times that on the spot. I shook my head. "This is show and tell. We're not shopping yet, but we're going to be injecting some life into your wardrobe—blue, lime, coral, yellow, pale pink."

She twitched with uncertainty. It took most women a while to get used to what they hadn't worn before. Imagine donning a new skin. For the rest of the morning we moved through the hangers, making sure everything fit properly. After the sixth pair of pants, she turned to me, eyebrows raised. "I guess there's no point in trying *every*—"

"Right. I'm sure you would have chucked out *anything* that wasn't right."

Her back stiffened suddenly. Her failed marriage was the elephant in the room.

"I can't fix your *life*," I continued, shaking my head back and forth slowly, "but I can fix your *wardrobe*—and it's a forward step."

She smiled more genuinely than before. We were beginning to connect. If that didn't happen, the job wouldn't be fun for either of us and I'd become the warden. She'd resent my authority, resent spending money on what I advised, and probably never wear anything I encouraged her to buy.

I moved from shrink brain back to closet brain. "You've

got your bottom half down pat, so let's concentrate on tops, jackets, and accessories. When we're done, you'll have snapshots of all the outfits we put together so there won't be any guesswork involved in looking perfect." I took out my schedule and looked for a day for us to shop. "I'm guessing you're a morning person."

"I'm up at five thirty."

"That must be morning somewhere."

She raised an eyebrow, and then smiled.

"I try to shop with clients when they're at their best. And I'll never push you beyond your comfort zone."

Some hit the wall after two hours. Some could go longer. Only teenagers could put up with an entire day of me ushering them in and out of dressing rooms with armloads of clothes, in spite of the rations I carried—dried fruit, nuts, and water, and, if the client wasn't overweight, bittersweet chocolate. And we never skipped lunch. She must have been reading my mind.

"Can you stay for a sandwich?"

It was almost two and I hadn't had anything since Grape-Nuts at dawn. Never mind hunger, the house was so fabulous I didn't want to leave.

We sipped San Pellegrino as her housekeeper fixed us shrimp salad sandwiches on croissants with TERRA chips and cranberry juice with lime. She set the tray down in the living room on a small French table between beige linen club chairs with down cushions. A white napkin, also linen, with embroidered initials was folded next to each celadon plate. Delicately etched glasses in a coordinating pale green held the juice. They looked Venetian.

It was so art directed. I wished for a missed chord,

something defying perfection. Tarnished silver, a blow-in card on the floor, some half-dead flowers, anything. But her life was styled like a photo shoot.

Like the letter?

My mind kept circling back to it. He might live in a house like this. He'd sit by a window staring at the ocean, or run on the beach for miles trying to get Caroline out of his head. He'd be the sensitive type, with good cheekbones and longish hair. I could see him behind the wheel of a vintage Porsche. He'd collect things like old travel books or antique maps and have a library of first editions. He traveled a lot. Money was never an object. Maybe he had a trust fund. At the very least, he was supplying me with rich fantasies. I tried to push thoughts of him away and bring myself back.

The living room was taupe and cream with antique Fortuny accent pillows and porcelain in moss, lime, and aubergine. A limestone floor with hues of beige and gray gave a cool elegance to the room. The chairs faced a large bay window framing a popsicle-blue sky that lent a perfect jolt of color to the room. Gentle waves softly washed up on the shore. Not a soul in sight. What a rarefied way of life. But somewhere along the way, Mary Alice Moriarity became blind to it. Circumstances had railroaded her. Her glorious ocean panorama could have been the brick wall of a neighboring building. She was living proof that money couldn't buy happiness.

"Your house is magnificent." I startled her. The compliment didn't seem to register. She was silent, but shook her head slightly. "It takes a long time to get over a relationship," I said, carefully venturing into her precarious world of loss and pain. Her eyes widened as though I had read her thoughts.

"It survived the building of this house," she said, pausing to remove a blue thread on the seat of the chair with her white, birdlike hand, "even though at one point I doubted it. But as soon as his Xanadu was finished, he started sleeping in a hovel in Greenwich Village with someone half his age. He 'found himself,'" she said as if something were lodged in her throat.

The stoic serenity of the woman who had greeted me was replaced by someone living between fury and pain. She told me about Richard, an investment banker she met at Wharton. A stay-at-home wife appealed to him, so she convinced herself she'd had her share of corporate America and resigned from a high-powered position in finance.

"It was fun at first," she said. "No schedules, no meetings, no business suits. I filled my days visiting antique stores and planning dinners." She learned bridge and joined a book club. On weekends they left the city. They flew to Newport, Aspen, the Florida Keys, and Bermuda. But after a few years, things changed. He lost interest in traveling with her. She lost interest in spending time with women who lunched. He started working late. Then he was away for weeks at a time, seeing clients.

"Of course, she went with him." She waved her hand as though it was pointless to go on.

"She was his *secretary*," she said, as if it were synonymous with *scullery maid*. "They just *clicked*." She stared into the distance for a long minute, her taut bottom lip almost quivering as she relived it. "Now I've been away from the work world for what…eight or nine years?" She held her hands out in a helpless gesture. "And everything changes.

You can't just pick up and go back." She reached for a pack of cigarettes on the table and then pushed them away in disgust. "I haven't smoked for twenty years and the other day I bought a pack. Can you believe that? That's where I am."

An H-bomb had gone off in her life, so yes, going back to smoking made as much sense as anything. After Greg, my filmmaker boyfriend from college, left my appetite went haywire and all I could swallow for breakfast was potato chips washed down with Coke. Finding your boyfriend in your bed with someone else can do that. Everything in life becomes hard to digest. I didn't share that with Mary Alice because I was a professional, or attempted to act like one. Anyway, I tried to keep the conversation on an up note.

"Would you like to do the same kind of work you were doing?"

She shook her head. "Actually, I'd like to do something totally different. I was thinking of starting a line of gourmet foods—upscale condiments, exotic teas." She crossed her arms over her chest as if she were protecting her business plan.

"So why don't you?"

"I may, I just have to get to that point."

"How long has he been gone?"

"Three months."

"Are you sure it's over?"

"He told me he wanted to marry her. He wanted to start over." She lifted her chin. "He said he felt as though he was never married." A flash of hurt hit her face like a lightning strike. It was one thing to tell someone you had stopped loving them, and another to negate their existence by saying your time together was meaningless.

Being smart and successful was useless at times. You lived under the illusion that you had the resources to handle whatever came your way. You had your network of friends and colleagues to support you. They could be counted on to drop off dinner or listen when you needed to vent. Then, out of the blue, life tested you in a way you never imagined, and you were exiled from the world, powerless to deflect the blows. Your choices were to surrender to the misery or to take action and seek distraction by doing things like changing your wardrobe so you could re-enter the world looking and feeling like you were a new breed of yourself, one who could cope. I didn't offer up my own supportive events. I was her advisor, not her drinking buddy.

"So you have to start over too."

She exhaled as she pushed back her plate. The sandwich was barely touched. The nourishment she needed didn't come from seafood.

"We'll work from the outside in."

She gazed at me with a hint of a smile. "One shawl at a time."

At least she still had a sense of humor. On the way to the door, I spotted a large abstract painting in the hallway. I hadn't noticed it when I'd walked in. Maybe I was too busy watching the Ridgebacks watch me. The canvas was nearly six feet high. Unlike everything else in the house, it was bursting with vibrant color and bold, energetic brushstrokes. The longer I looked at it, the more it drew me in. As I was about to ask about it, the dogs started barking. Mary Alice looked out the window.

"It's just the gardener," she said, as a truck pulled up.

On the drive home I thought about Mary Alice's house,

her wardrobe, her life, and the adjustment after a divorce. I thought about estrangement and my mind went back to the letter, now my North Star. How long were they together? Had they gotten engaged? Married? How long since they were apart? Was he still writing her letters? Had she answered any of them? Or were there others, strewn around the city, abandoned in taxis or in trash cans, or with cross marks that said "return to sender"?

I thought back to a newspaper story about an interior designer who helped clients redecorate their homes after their spouses were gone—"Personal Style, Unleashed by Divorce," was the headline. The designer dubbed the new look "revenge décor," because the designs were based wholly on the newly single client's style, not subject to input from a partner with opposing tastes.

Mary Alice didn't have to redesign her home, but she had a parallel mission: to redesign her life and start to express her inner self, starting with her wardrobe. She had to open herself to life again, and fill it with brightness and joy, starting with what touched her skin. She was isolated in a palace on the ocean with only the maid, two guard dogs, and a dark closet. I thought about Caroline. Had she had moved on and found someone else? Or, like Mary Alice, was she alone sleeping with just her memories?

chapter three

Most of my clients didn't live in mansions overlooking the ocean. More often home was a snug Manhattan apartment with closets as tight as crawl spaces and unobstructed views of an airshaft. Beth, a newly divorced real estate agent, had recently moved into a one-bedroom apartment. She had acquired a new address; now she needed a fresh identity.

Home decoration wasn't something she seriously grappled with. I saw it as soon as I walked in. To be generous, her style was eclectic. So was the state of her closet. "Resist the temptation to pare down your wardrobe before I get there," I told her on the phone. "What you have tells me how you see yourself."

No one had to be embarrassed by the skeletons in their closet. We all fell prey to fantasy behind dressing room curtains. As Jerry Seinfeld said it, injecting his droll humor: "Buying clothes is always tricky. But when there's loud music playing, it really throws your judgment. You look at stuff like, 'Hey, if there was a cool party and I was a cool guy, this might be a cool shirt.' You get it home, there's no music, there's no party, and you're not a cool guy. You're the same chump, seventy-five bucks lighter."

Beth's closet said one word to me: Sybil. It had a multiple personality disorder.

"I thought all the styles represented different parts of me," she said, trying to defend the chaos.

It was six in the evening and her workday was over. She answered the door in a royal-blue velour tracksuit that highlighted her poochy belly. Her flip-flops were the same regatta blue. Anchors away. The vamp toenail polish didn't flatter her stubby toes or her milky white skin, but the pedicure was glossy and chip free, wafting out the heavy girl message: A part of me *is* perfect.

"We're going to give you a strong, dynamic image," I said. "The pastiche of styles you've collected are adding confusion"—*not to mention a hippie, middle-aged look*—"instead of projecting the secure image of a professional woman who's sexy and now single."

Since her divorce, her diversions were shopping and eating. The payback was a jump of thirty pounds and a wardrobe with more styles than Ben & Jerry's had flavors. Plus, she had a thin wardrobe and a fat one. That explained the flouncy skirts, baggy caftans, and the flapping Chico's hide-behinds.

So we purged. Piles for the consignment shop and the garbage, dumping "good deals," those expensive bargains.

"You have six months to fit into the thin clothes," I said, "otherwise they're out." Closet space was too valuable to waste; it was like real estate. She frowned as the discard pile grew in opposition to what remained on the rods.

I prattled on as I pruned. My job was not only to improve her wardrobe but also to help her feel good about herself and sparkle up her day, so I edited my comments, going for honesty laced with kindness.

"My God," Beth said, looking through what was left in her closet after we got through. "It's so neat, so organized."

"How do you feel about it now?" I asked her.

"More in control," she said. "I mean I would wear everything, everything that's left. It feels…organized," she said.

"We put your wardrobe on a diet," I said. I didn't finish the rest of the sentence, but she did: "And now it's time for me to go on one."

Sometimes just tidying up someone's wardrobe was enough to push them to do what they wanted to do, but couldn't motivate themselves to on their own. It also helped that they paid for my services, because it made them feel they had to get as much as possible back from their investment.

How I finessed these situations was of endless fascination to my best friend, Jennelle, a wardrobe work in progress. I waited for the day she'd turn her back on the near-death experience of a career in banking, never mind the 401(k) and medical coverage up the gazoo.

She'd grinned impishly. "What do you say if someone tries on slacks that make her rear end look like the back of a bus?"

"I'm not happy with the fit."

"And if someone's wardrobe's a total disaster?"

"You're much more attractive than your clothing."

• • •

After Beth saw the outfits I put together for her, she came around to my way of thinking. After her wardrobe lobotomy, she not only started a diet, she asked me for the names of a hairdresser and a makeup artist. Six weeks later, she sent me a JPEG of herself in one of the outfits we had left in her closet. She was twenty pounds lighter.

"The new me!" she said. And then in brackets, "Do you know of a good plastic surgeon? Must tighten the neck now."

I was used to that. To my clients, I was an authority on everything. One night when Jennelle and I were having dinner, my cell rang. A client heading out of town asked me if I knew where she could board her cat.

"You're the fixer," Jennelle said, flatly.

"No, I'm a clothes consultant."

"You become their life coach," she said. "You're so *supportive* of everyone else, so why are you so hard on yourself?"

"Dysfunctional people are like that."

I didn't share that I carried the letter in my bag like a talisman I needed to keep close. The next day, in fact, I left an afternoon to pursue LW, as I began to think of the letter writer. The letter was signed "Jordan" and had a return address. Only, Jordan had a big place in which to hide. His lower Fifth Avenue high-rise had thirty-two floors.

And the name—so achingly ordinary. If only it were eccentric or catchy. Cormac. Guerin, Campion, Joaquin, Elvis, Flash, Siegfried, Jett, even Wolf—not that I could imagine falling for one. Still, Jordan could write. And he didn't give up. He wasn't a pushover and neither was I.

But before I stood outside his white brick building in full view of the doorman, addressing every man who entered or exited, "Excuse me, Jordan?" I went online and checked the reverse telephone directory. Although anyone with an unlisted number wouldn't be included, it was a start. I found eight people who either had the first name Jordan or the initial *J*. At seven thirty in the evening, when most people were home from work, I started calling.

"Excuse me, I'm trying to reach Jordan."

A pregnant pause. "Which one?"

"How many are there?"

"My husband and my son."

"Your son." Another pause.

"He's seven…can I help?"

I mumbled an apology and hung up. If Jordan senior was the writer, his wife was the last person I wanted to talk to about the letter. I forged ahead.

"Bartholomew residence." The housekeeper.

"Excuse me, I'm looking for someone named Jordan, if I have the right number," I said, like a twit. "I think he's about thirty, is he there?"

"Jordan? Mr. Jordan, no, he away at college. He no thirty, he eighteen and he away at college."

A college boy capable of writing a letter like that? Not likely. "I'll try him there," I muttered, quickly disconnecting. I'd gone through seven of the eight names on the list, including a Jordana who said she had just moved to New York from the South. There was one number left and I had to get lucky. Jordan Johnson. Only that time, I didn't get a person.

"I'm sorry you've gotten the machine, but please don't hang up," said the smooth male voice. "Take a moment to leave me your name and number and I'll get back to you...I will."

Some primitive part of my brain fired, filling me with certainty. It had nothing to do with logic. Number eight was LW. After I left my number, I changed my cell ring to vibra-ring, made sure it was fully charged, and became obsessed with checking my messages.

But he didn't call that night. Or the next day. Or the day after.

So I began to ponder the spectrum of possible explanations: Out of town. Hospitalized. Deceased. Uninterested. Careless and lost the number. Dyslexic. Moved in with her. Check the *Times* for an announcement. Should I leave a second message? And then the scenario I rehearsed if he ever did call.

"Hello, Jordan? Listen, I know this sounds so ridiculous, but I was in a cab and I almost lost my life when it was hit by a reckless limo driver, but anyway, as I was scooping up Miracle Bras from the floor of the cab I found your letter and I immediately fell for you, never mind that Caroline person." He'd assume I was phoning from a locked cell in a psychiatric hospital. I had to do better.

"Hi, is this Jordan?" (Breezy tone.) "You don't know me, but I found something that belongs to you, or really, belongs to Caroline. No, I don't know *her* either, but I happened to discover a letter you wrote to her on the floor of a taxi. No, I know you didn't write it *on* the floor of the taxi, I just found it there, but anyway—How did I find *you*? Easy, really. I just took a week off from work, canceled a Caribbean vacation, and scoured the reverse telephone directory, not to mention getting ready to stand watch outside your building for hours waiting for every male resident to come home so

I could interrogate him."

No, I wouldn't rehearse. If he called, he called. If he didn't, it wasn't meant to be. I'd find a real person, not a ghost.

I slumped back onto the sofa and watched *The Year of Living Dangerously*, an ancient video that Greg in his rush to leave had somehow forgotten to pack. When the phone rang it didn't register at first. I was in the thrall of exotic Jakarta in 1965 before the overthrow of Sukarno, where a handsome and naïve journalist named Guy (Mel Gibson) meets and falls for Jilly (Sigourney Weaver), who works in the British embassy as a spook. She's torn between feelings for Mel and wanting to get him out of the country safely before fighting breaks out while at the same time keeping secret government reports to herself. But the phone broke my concentration.

"Hey, wanna get some Chinese?"

Not the dashing Jordan—far, far from it.

Arnie, my nebbish of a neighbor from upstairs. Arnie played a number of roles in my life: friend, dog-sitter, and surrogate date for events where I needed to show up with a man because everybody else would be with a date or a husband. Arnie was my walker, as they say of the usually gay men who accompany society babes to events. Only Arnie wasn't gay, he was just…well…Arnie-ish. Even though he had good hair, he refused to shell out more than ten bucks for a decent haircut, so he looked like he needed work. Still, he was helpful. He showed up. When I was sick, he thought to bring soup. He had a kind side, a goodness (albeit sometimes deep down), and because he lived one floor above me and I could virtually track his movements by the sounds of the pipes and the squeaks in the floor, it felt like we were as close as I was with Harry—minus the cuddling.

I had learned long ago that there was no talking to him about clothes. Despite my offers to take him to the designer showrooms where he could get clothes at about fifty percent off, Arnie preferred to go to Century 21, where he managed to unearth peculiar off-labels, coming home with things that were forgettable at best, even though the whole point of the store was to track down designer bargains. The sad truth was that Arnie wouldn't recognize an Armani jacket if he fell over it.

"Great," I said. "I'd love Chinese." We did share that bond, either ordering out every week or two or going down to Chinatown on Sunday nights to places we loved, like the cheapo Prosperity Dumpling on Eldridge Street, or Tasty Hand-Pulled Noodles on Doyers Street.

I had forgotten about dinner and my refrigerator was filled with leftovers of uncertain origin. "But let's eat here, I'm waiting for a call."

"Sage…Greg isn't going to call."

"Arnie," I mimicked his dyspeptic tone, "I'm not waiting for Greg, I'm waiting for Jordan."

"Jordan? Michael Jordan?"

"Cute. No, actually Jordan Johnson. I think that's his name, but I don't know for sure."

"Run that by me again."

Over our moo shu vegetables, I showed him the letter.

"They're probably back together again," he said, drowning his vegetables in hoisin sauce before rolling the pancake so fat that it resembled a giant stogie. "You're wasting your time."

He scarfed down everything on his plate plus my

leftovers, never mind that he had just complained about the food being greasy.

"You've been around Greg too long, 'cause now you're making this little film in your head and you're probably way off-base."

I stared hard out the window and looked back at him accusingly. "There's nothing wrong with making little films in your head." What I really wanted to tell him at that point was to screw himself. Who was *he* to talk? He was consumed with Gilda, the matchless beauty he had hooked up with his freshman year of college, seven years ago. He was forever fantasizing that one day she would call him and come back. Rather unlikely since she had gotten married, had twins, and moved to Jersey and they hadn't as much as emailed in years.

"Okay," he said with his signature smirk. "So what are you going to say to Shakespeare if he does call? You got the hots for him because he has a hard-on for some babe who walked out on him?"

Clearly, Arnie didn't have a romantic bone in his body.

I shook my head dismissively. "I really haven't rehearsed it. When the phone rings, I suppose I'll just know. Fate put the letter in my path, and fate will take care of what happens from here on out."

"Fate?" Arnie snickered, reaching for a fortune cookie. "That might work." He broke it open and removed the paper. He laughed. "I love this crap. Listen to this: 'Hurry up and learn patience.'"

He gestured toward me. "What's yours?"

I broke the cookie and held together the pieces of the small white rectangle I'd inadvertently ripped in two. "No land without stones—or meat without bones." Not exactly what I'd hoped for.

He shrugged. "Rough road ahead."

And then the phone rang. We both turned to it. He got up and pretended to dribble a basketball, suddenly pivoting as though he were about to make a jump shot.

"Could be your guy."

chapter four

When the phone rang at ten fifteen, just after I opened that ridiculous fortune cookie, it seemed preordained that Jordan would call. I answered in my most seductive phone voice.

Phony as it was, I had several telephone voices, as do most people, even if they won't admit it. Anyone who knew me could tell if I was talking to my mother, Arnie, Jennelle, a client, or someone I was interested in sleeping with. Can you guess which voice I answered with? Clearly, though, the whole Chinese restaurant fortune cookie copy department was now having a Buddha-sized belly laugh at my expense.

"Frank?"

"Frank?"

"Frank," he repeated.

"There's no one here by that name." I lapsed into my voice for telephone solicitors. "You obviously have the wrong number."

"No Frank?"

"No," I hissed. "And it's after ten on a weeknight.

Even if he was here, he'd be dead asleep." I hung up and it rang again. I let it go to voicemail. The caller didn't leave a message. Not for me. Or Frank.

• • •

It was one of those weekday mornings when the entire transit system was out of whack. This time someone having a psychotic fit had flung himself on the tracks at Union Square. When he refused to budge, backup police were called and trains were halted, paralyzing movement across much of the city. As I waited for the situation to be resolved, more and more people filled the platform until it was packed like Times Square on New Year's. Only there was no revelry, just menacing looks at the loudspeaker farting out indecipherable sounds intermittently to explain something. I headed for the exit to hunt for a cab. As I was walking up the staircase in the middle of a thick crowd of grumbling commuters who had made the same decision, I felt something alive in my pocket. I shrieked. People around me stared momentarily and then resumed their climb without a second glance, having had their fill of psychotic behavior for one morning. It was the vibra-ring of my cell.

"What?" I said, in despair.

"You called *me*." He had a velvety voice with a trace of an English accent. Jude Law-ish.

"Who *is* this?" I asked impatiently.

"You called Jordan, didn't you?"

I bounded to the top of the staircase, walked toward a building to get away from the crowds, and then crouched down. My skin prickled underneath my sweater.

"Yes," I said, trying to meld my clipped, irritated voice into a more appealing one. "Yes...I did."

"Well then," he said, sounding almost amused, "what is it?"

"Here goes..." I exhaled for effect. "I found a letter you wrote—a love letter—and well, I—I had to talk to the man who wrote it because...to be honest...it was one of the most beautiful, seductive love letters I've ever read."

Silence. I held the phone back from my ear to make sure we hadn't gotten disconnected. The way things were going that morning, it wouldn't have surprised me if the connection broke and I never heard from him again. But it looked like we were still connected. I let out my breath. No doubt he was convinced I was out of my mind.

"I didn't expect this..."

"I realize it's strange."

"Well, I'm intrigued," he said, finally. "If this isn't a New York story...a perfect stranger calling because she read a love letter. Listen, I've got a crazy day...but do you think we could meet for a drink later on?"

"A drink?" The village idiot with echolalia.

"Wine, perhaps...champagne?"

He was already laughing at me.

"We could meet around seven, if you're free. How about Rise?"

"Yes...okay...what time?"

"Seven?"

"Fine." Seven. He had already said seven. I hung up and headed to my appointment, only to come to my senses. I knew my way around the city pretty well—I had lived here for my entire life. But Rise? I had never heard of it. Was it a restaurant? A bar? It could be a church, a courtroom (*all rise…*). I'd call the authority on all places drink-related. I speed-dialed Jennelle.

"Have you ever heard of a place called Rise?" No surprise that I neglected formalities.

"Rise? Or R-I-C-E?"

Christ, did he say Rice? Was it a Chinese restaurant? A macrobiotic dive? "I think Rise. Or maybe ricin." *No, that was the god-awful poison.* "It's got to be a bar or something and I'm supposed to meet someone there for a drink but I've got no clue what the hell it is or where."

"Wait." Keys clicking. "It a bar at the Ritz-Carlton Hotel on the fourteenth floor," she said. "Wall Street area." There was a pause. "Ooh la la…it looks like quite a romantic little place. Listen to this: 'The Sugar and Spice package provides a lovers' escape complete with a passport to indulgence; includes couples massage and entry to the exclusive Chocolate Bar.'"

"*WHAT?*" So first I fantasized about Wall Street getting quiet at the end of the workday and him trying to lure me into a room in the hotel after we met for a quick drink up on the fourteenth floor, and then I thought about massages and the chocolate bar and I started to sweat. Why couldn't we meet somewhere down on the ground, not up in the clouds?

I mean, *Rise?* What kind of name was that? Maybe he would, that's why he thought of it. Maybe he was a sicko. What had I gotten myself into? And Wall Street? Unless you both worked in the financial district, why would you suggest having a drink down there? It was deserted at night.

What people outside of Manhattan failed to understand was that people in Manhattan dreaded going far (except to Europe) for anything. That's why we paid the absurd prices we did. Everyone should live and work in the same zip code, someone smart once said.

"Fuck. Thanks, Jennelle."

"Who are you meeting? You sound like a madwoman."

Jennelle was my human Richter scale, ever-ready to give me a reading on the seismic events in my life. "My cell's running out of juice. It's complicated," I said. "I'll call you later."

I wanted to meet Jordan, but not in lower Manhattan at a hotel bar that had a name like an erection. I called him back.

"Jordan, it's Sage." I put a smile in my voice. "Listen, I'm sure Rise is a lovely place, but I forgot that I've got to be uptown this afternoon and I don't think I'll be able to make it downtown in time. Could we meet someplace up *here?*"

"Hmmm."

Was he stretching or considering the uptown possibilities? Maybe he was in the middle of making love to Caroline or some other conquest.

"How about the Carlyle?" he said, finally.

"Good...see you at seven." I was about to hang up when I heard, "Wait. How will I recognize you?"

"Five eight, shoulder-length reddish-brown hair, green eyes." I looked at what I was wearing. "A green Chanel jacket with jeans."

"Hmmm," he said again, this time with a smile in *his* voice. "I'll find you."

I spent most of the morning with a client. I was calm and professional. I had all the answers to her wardrobe woes and she felt she could count on me.

"I'd like to be like you," she said, almost worshipful. "Stylish, self-assured, in touch with what flatters you

37

and what doesn't."

If she only knew.

As soon as I was out the door, my veneer of self-assurance cracked like thin ice. To get ready to meet Jordan I canceled my next appointment—*I'm so sorry, I've got these flulike symptoms*—something I hated to do not only because it meant lying but also because I was tempting fate. But the upcoming rendezvous with LW put me in overdrive. An EKG right then would have shown the blips, bells, and bongs of a pinball machine.

I entered my closet, pulling out tops, bottoms, shoes, and jewelry, trying this and that, tossing the rejects to the floor. Like the writer who faces twenty-six keys on the computer and knows all that's necessary for a bestseller is arriving at the right combination, somewhere in the closet was the right match.

You have one chance to make a serious impression. I repeatedly told my clients that. I settled on a slim black YSL skirt, a find from David Owens Vintage Clothing on Orchard Street, black alligator slingbacks that I bought for next to nothing at Buffalo Exchange in Williamsburg, and a three-quarter-sleeve white cashmere Versace sweater with a scoop neck that I bought back when I was in college at Michael's Resale, a consignment shop on Madison Avenue where Jackie Kennedy was said to have dumped her castoffs.

The overall look was revealing, but refined. A bold, silver Elsa Peretti cuff that molded snugly around my wrist, and dangling silver mesh earrings that moved with me. Yin-yangish, I thought.

I spent an excruciating amount of time on my hair so it fell in right, applying "product," as my hair colorist dubbed the styling cream (as in, "Do you want *product?*") that she slicked on the roots and ends with lightning speed to give it body and shine. I wore it down instead of back, the way I did for work. Light foundation, eyeliner pencil, and lipstick blotted to a stain. I picked a black Chanel purse and a short white wool Prada jacket. I waved to Harry and locked the door behind me.

I walked to Third Avenue and lifted my arm to flag down a cab. There were usually people at all points of the intersection poised to halt the first cab, as if they were on a reality show and getting a cab meant survival.

Only not then. A cab pulled up instantaneously and that does *not* happen. I was going to be disgustingly early. I sat back hoping for a tie-up or street construction but no, not a pothole or even a nick. We moved faster than a bobsled on a luge course. I had the driver drop me a few blocks before the hotel and I walked the rest of the way, whiling away time looking into stores on Madison Avenue, stopping at Zitomer, a pharmacy/department store known for exotic toiletries, European underwear, an amazing collection of hard-to-find goodies like peel-and-stick bras and deodorant-removing sponges, natural cures like Vocalzone throat pastilles that I bought for a client who was a singer and lost her voice, and SinEcch—capsules of *Arnica montana*—that I found for a client who had lingering bruises after a facelift and had an upcoming event she had to look perfect for.

7:10. My pencil-thin heels rat-tat-tatted across the polished black granite lobby floor. Only then did I remember telling Jordan that I was wearing a green Chanel jacket and jeans. Fabulous. He'd now know I went to the trouble of changing. So much for my hectic day.

I made my way to Bemelmans Bar, an intimate space known for the whimsical murals done by the creator of the Madeline children's books, Ludwig Bemelmans. The story goes that he was a guest at the hotel and painted them as a form of barter because he couldn't afford his bill. Despite the child-friendly nature of the art, the bar is touted as one of New York's most romantic spots. And it lives up to its reputation. It's lush, leathery, and dimly lit—that soft golden light that airbrushes away imperfections. Dressing rooms lit that way turned you into a swan and cost you serious money. Day or night, you can count on seeing celebrities here. One evening I met a friend there and Paul McCartney walked in. The piano player wasted no time segueing into "Penny Lane."

As if arriving in another outfit weren't bad enough, I got there before Jordan did. And I hate that. "I'm meeting someone," I murmured to the maître d'. I was seated at a small table along a dark leather banquette. Not counting the bartender, I was the only one in the room who was alone. No book, no newspaper. I filled the minutes staring at my phone, but really dissecting my life.

Sage Parker, a thirty-four-year-old unmarried closet consultant, recently ditched by her filmmaker boyfriend who preferred an anorexic French actress devoid of fashion savvy, was sitting in a bar waiting to meet a total stranger who wrote a letter she unearthed on the filthy floor of a cab. She went to great lengths to track the writer, making blind calls to strangers in the phone book, canceling client appointments, and finally spending hours in her closet to come up with the right outfit.

There it was. I uncrossed my legs and crossed them again. Dress up and sit alone in a bar and whoosh, you're a hooker. I avoided extended eye contact with men in the room and pretended to study the murals. I glanced to my left when I sensed someone approaching. He was tall and powerfully built, with a ponytail and wearing a long black leather coat. Jordan? Not the way I'd pictured him. He scanned the crowd and waved to someone across the room before he headed that way.

Not Jordan. Good. Ponytails rarely worked unless the man was under thirty and a rich Italian with soulful eyes, perhaps the black sheep of a prominent family. Otherwise: drug czar, hit man, or bouncer.

Back to the murals. Someone else came close. Not Jordan. A waiter, unless Jordan masqueraded as one to check me out before committing himself. I wasn't losing my ground or anything. More mural scrutiny until I looked up again. I was sure it was the omnipresent waiter, but this time, someone about six foot two in a wonderful suit was smiling down at me. Very good eyes and an easy smile.

"Sage?"

I looked back at him, aware of the atoms of attraction bombarding each other.

"Yes." He pulled out the chair opposite me and sat down.

"Nice Chanel jacket," he said, deadpan.

I flashed him my most radiant smile. "It would have been an hour ago."

He was critically handsome with beautifully cut dark hair, a fine, straight nose, and a searching look in his deep-set, coffee-colored eyes, if the light wasn't distorting them. Impeccable fit to the navy gabardine suit over a deep blue shirt and striped navy tie. I could have improved just a mite on the tie, but whatever. He was broad-shouldered, elegant. Large, graceful hands like a surgeon and perfect nails, and I was thinking about the possibilities.

"What are you drinking?" he asked. "Can I get you another?" My glass was almost empty, I realized. It had been six hours since lunch. I didn't do well drinking on an empty stomach.

"Chardonnay, thanks."

He ordered a gin martini. We sat silently for an awkward few seconds taking each other's measure. The drinks came and after a quick "Salut," he looked at me with a guilty smile. "So you were intrigued by a love letter."

I sipped the wine, rotating the stem between my fingers. "It's just not the kind of thing men do anymore... And anyway, you write so well."

"Actually, I don't," he said, rubbing the back of his neck, "but whatever."

"What do you do for a living?" It wouldn't have surprised me to hear he wrote novels. Maybe he was a publisher, an actor, or a pilot. Too well-dressed to be a journalist.

"Mergers and acquisitions." He shook his head, almost in disbelief himself. "And you?"

"I help people get dressed," I said, feeling the wine supersaturating my blood.

"How's that?" He tilted his head to the side with a half smile. Was the alcohol working on him too, or was he just naturally cocky?

"I'm a wardrobe consultant. If you needed help with your wardrobe I'd go through your closet with you and tell you what to keep and what to throw out. Then we'd go shopping." I studied his face. Some people were amused by how I spent my time. Or envious. Others thought it was stupid and shallow. Like an astute businessman, he held his feelings in check.

"You'd come into my closet?" He leaned forward, giving it more intimacy and danger than it merited. "And how much would that service cost?"

I narrowed my eyes, aware of my breathing. "It would depend on how long it took," I said, slowly reaching for my drink. Why was this conversation starting to sound like something it wasn't? For diversion, or at least a blood sugar boost, it would have helped to have some snack food. Pretzels or Goldfish crackers, but there was just the plump Spanish olive stuffed with red pimento speared on his toothpick, and I wasn't about to reach across the table and slide it off into my mouth.

"It's about clothing and self-image...it's not what you're thinking."

"How do you know what I'm thinking?"

"Hmmm," I said, mimicking him, "just my sixth sense. So you're English," I said, coming up with a great non sequitur.

He nodded with a knowing smile.

"And you live here now?"

"No, I live in London most of the time. I'm here for business a few months of the year, though. And you're from New York?"

"Yes."

"And you're single?"

I nodded again. "And you?"

He paused for a moment. "Married."

Slap.

"My wife's at home," he said.

I tried to show no emotion, but I felt stung. He wasn't

wearing a wedding band; I had checked the moment he sat down. I couldn't deny the attraction, and now all my detective work, my hours of fantasy, not to mention all that time in my closet and the canceled client appointment were for nothing. The game was over. For once, Arnie was so, so right. The whole thing was like a movie I made up in my head. If I didn't know better, I'd think that Greg the wretch had staged it all for the cinematic possibilities.

"So why did you ask to meet me for a drink? What was the point?" I tried to keep my voice neutral, hoping he didn't see my cheeks starting to flush.

"I was intrigued, obviously," he said. "You called me, I didn't call you. It was unusual, to say the least, to get a phone call like that. Can you blame me for wondering who you were?"

"No...yes...I—I don't know. But now we've met and it's getting late and I haven't eaten, and you're married, so before I'm blotto from two glasses of wine on an empty stomach"—I pushed out my chair—"I'd better be going."

I was about to leave when I realized I hadn't asked him about Caroline. Clearly he had had an affair with her. Maybe that was his pattern. He was strikingly handsome; how easy it would be for him to take lovers with his wife an ocean away. He was a serial adulterer, no doubt. Women flocked to his door and he had his pick, secure that he'd never be found out. Wonderful sexual adventures for a month or two, then he'd return home—the faithful husband. He wined them, dined them, and if someone should turn her back on him before he was through with her, he'd get out his Montblanc and dash off a heart-wrenching missive about how he couldn't live without her.

I waited a moment while he signed the check. I knew one thing: I wasn't going to be his latest conquest. I stood up and put on my jacket.

"Don't run off," he said, tucking his wallet into a back pocket, as he saw me buttoning my jacket. "Please. We'll get some dinner. I won't follow you home or anything. No strings attached…I'd just like to get to know you."

"I have to go…but one last question. Whatever happened to Caroline?"

He narrowed his eyes. "Why do you want to know?"

"Well, in your letter…you sounded so desperately in love with her…I mean, that was the whole point, wasn't it? So I wondered."

"It's over," he said, shaking his head dismissively. "It's history."

"I see."

He looked at me strangely. I stood up. All around us, sitting at the intimate café tables, were couples who seemed to be basking in each other's company without any labored backstory. After drinks and a light dinner, they'd either jump in their limos and head home or go upstairs to their two-thousand-dollar suites with fresh flowers and spectacular Central Park views to spend the night in king-size beds, in each other's arms.

There were 8.2 million people in New York. It was the most densely populated city in North America. Was it too much to hope that I would meet one man, one *single* man whom I could love, or was I destined to hit the online dating sites for the rest of my life and go off for coffee after endless coffee? Most women found someone. Yes, even women who *didn't* know how to dress. Women who wore cheap, badly fitting, unflattering clothes. Women with no fashion or style sense whatsoever. Women who were too fat or too thin. Kmart shoppers. Socialites. Low-end, high-end. Everybody. *Any*body. They had husbands, lovers, dates. They didn't resort to hunting down perfect strangers for companionship. They met men the usual ways. They didn't comb the floors of taxis like desperate bag ladies and have high hopes that perfect strangers would transport them.

I was pathetic and loveless—well-dressed outside, but peel away my designer layers and I was a designer clone of Beth, who had OD'd on fried chicken legs and seven-layer cake, trying to shop and eat her way out of despair by buying more and more shapeless, hideous fat clothes to hide behind. I rushed to the door without looking behind me. Well-dressed people strolled by, enjoying the night air on their way home.

"Sage, wait," he called out, catching up to me. "You don't know the whole story. I owe you an explanation. This wasn't…fair."

"Fair?" I hesitated. Since when was life fair? "It's fine, really." I held my arm up and again, like in the movies and almost never in real life, a cab pulled up and I got in without turning back or searching the floor for buried treasures.

chapter five

After *A Tale of Two Cities* and *David Copperfield*, I'd start *War and Peace*, unless I could unearth a heftier doorstopper, more demanding of my time. No social life, barely any male friends. I was a wardrobe mistress, a drone. I lifted hems, inserted shoulder pads, pulled up panty hose, nipped and tucked clothing, and shopped like a robotic consumer, a Stepford buyer. I dressed other people to live better lives while my own was as vacuous as an empty walk-in.

At least I had Harry. Like two lost souls whose lives intersected at their moments of greatest need, we nourished each other's existence.

I found Harry at the ACC, the Animal Care and Control on East 110th Street where I spent an afternoon working for New York Cares, a group that sends volunteers to needy venues around the city. Another time I volunteered at the pediatric ward of a hospital and read children stories, played games, and talked and listened to whoever needed to talk. Another time I helped pick up trash in Central Park. That particular Sunday, I took the 6 train to 116th Street and Lexington Avenue and then walked down to the New York City–run shelter to walk dogs. It was therapy for me, an effort to get a toehold on life after my social life crashed like a geriatric hard drive.

Harry's previous owner went overseas and couldn't take him so he was abandoned at the shelter, confined to a space the size of a small cubby. It had a gray concrete floor and bars on the outside. All Harry had to his name was a single chew toy. I walked him around the neighborhood and he tugged excitedly, going this way and that, sniffing everything around him, excited to be free of his cage. He tracked the scent of marinara sauce and tried to walk into an Italian restaurant. Diners looked up, surprised. Everyone laughed. I thought about ordering veal and peppers to go, but I wasn't sure how well it mixed with kibble.

After I took him back to his cage, he crouched down, dropping his head between his paws like a rag doll. He stared up at me with his large, moist, brown eyes. I started to leave, and then turned to look at him again. He was still staring. I walked back to the cage and kneeled down. He licked my fingers through the bars.

"Harry, oh God, Harry," I said. He didn't answer, but his eyes didn't leave mine either, so that sealed the deal. I wanted him. He wanted me. Why couldn't real-life relationships be that simple, honest, and direct?

I filled out all the paperwork. I gave references and a description of the type of home I'd be sharing with him. I hung around until everything checked out. They attached a blue leash to his blue collar.

"Harry, you're going to your forever home," the shelter

volunteer said to him as he opened his cage, leading him out to a new, free life.

I took Harry home like a new baby in the back seat of a cab. We went directly to Canine Styles, an upscale dog boutique on Lexington Avenue where I picked out a leopard-print velvet bed and half a dozen toys, including a tire, a rubber high-heeled shoe, and three squirrels inside a furry tree trunk. I picked out a red plaid leash and another that was black leather with silver stars, and then liver trainer chews and Carnivore Kisses duck treats, and then ordered a bag of dog food from a nearby store and we started our life together. I half expected to hear the first few bars of "We've Only Just Begun" when we walked out into the street together like newlyweds.

As wonderful a companion as Harry turned out to be, my hormones sometimes told me to look for another male, one who perambulated on two feet. So I did while I kept busy with new clients whose needs spanned the spectrum.

The latest was a criminal lawyer who didn't want to show up in court in the four-thousand-dollar suits that filled his closet. He needed help picking out pieces that would make him look more like a man of the people. Our first stop was H&M, followed by Zara on Lexington and 59th Street, and then Nepenthes, on West 38th Street.

Then there was the ad executive who wrote copy for cutting-edge electronics and wanted to look more hip for client presentations. Since he had a kind of chunky build, and I knew it would be hard to find off-the-rack suits to fit him, I hired a Carmel cab for the afternoon and we zoomed down to Varet Street in Brooklyn to see Martin Greenfield, one of New York's best tailors.

I was also spending hours with Mary Alice. In just two shopping sessions we hit the Donna Karan showroom where I knew a saleswoman, Loro Piana on Madison where I wished I knew someone, a sprinkling of Madison Avenue boutiques, and Scoop on Third Avenue, for casual tops and pants. Then we got on the 6 train at 77th Street and Lexington (the only way to get downtown fast), and went down to Soho to AllSaints on Broadway for one of their edgy cocktail dresses.

That didn't count the online sites we hit, like TheOutnet. com, where I found a Halston Heritage bag for half of what it cost in Bloomingdale's, and yoox.com, where I found a cute Marc Jacobs bag in a killer shade of green for next to nothing. It wasn't that Mary Alice was looking to save money—it was just that I enjoyed chasing bargains, wherever I could find them, and I got her into the game.

Not that she got away cheap. Just *cheaper.* I lost count of the thousands she shelled out on sweaters, scarves and accessories. But it was worth it. Her new wardrobe made a striking difference in her appearance.

I turned to her one day when she was dressed head to toe in everything we had bought together and smiled. "You look cool, totally cool."

She blushed. "Cool? No one ever said that to me before. I was never cool." She actually held her head up higher and smiled, a real thousand-megawatt smile.

Younger too, I wanted to add, but didn't, because she might take it the wrong way. But she did look younger and looser. I grinned. "Amazing what you can get out of a few new schmattes."

I also suspected that Mary Alice enjoyed getting out

and having company. Actually, we'd become good friends. In a rare departure from her preoccupation with her broken marriage, she turned to me one day during lunch at Atlantic Grill on the Upper East Side.

"Are you seeing anyone?"

"Not at the moment." She studied me as I pushed my bay scallops around the plate. Then, as if a dam broke, I told her about the letter. "He was completely stunning. The man could have played the next James Bond." I paused to examine my nails. "So I guess it should come as no surprise that he was married."

"At least he owned up to it." Her eyes flickered with interest. "Where's the letter?"

"Home somewhere," I lied. I'd never admit I kept it in my bag like a good luck charm. We continued chatting and suddenly her face froze.

"Mary Alice, what is it?" Her eyes followed someone across the room. "Richard," she said, coldly. "And he's with *her*."

"Can I look?"

He was tall, with the paunch of a man who had salad as a side. Half bald, wearing a navy cashmere topcoat. A blonde with shoulder-length hair was next to him. Thirty, maybe. Bright-eyed newscaster type with a decent face, but no fashion savvy. White coat over a cheap purple blouse.

Mary Alice made a choking sound in the back of her throat. "Isn't she vile?"

"Should I slip her my card?"

She stared off into the distance, and quickly rebounded. Her hand shot up to summon the waiter. I picked up my bag, thinking we'd scoot for the door once he brought us the check.

"Merlot," she said, reminding me of Anne Bancroft in *The Graduate*. "Leave it at the bar for me." When he walked off, she turned to me. "Go to the bar and wait for the drink. Walk over to Richard's table when you have it. I'll be there."

I squeezed my eyes shut. "Why are you doing this?"

"It'll be *fun*," she said, brightly. "Don't you think?"

"Rethink this," I said, calmly.

"Go on now, he's pouring the wine."

I made my way to the bar and picked up the drink. I turned and headed toward the table. Mary Alice headed toward the back as if she were going to the ladies' room. She stopped, feigning surprise when she got to Richard's table. A small smile crossed her face as she chatted. I walked over and joined her.

"Sage," she said, raising a hand to pat me on the shoulder. *Swoosh*—the drink flew, turning the front of the girl's white coat pink.

"Jesus CHRIST!" Richard yelled, his voice stopping conversation at other tables. "WHAT THE HELL IS WRONG WITH YOU?"

"Oh my God, I'm so sorry," Mary Alice said. "Let me get club soda."

Richard jumped up and pulled the girl out of her seat, stabbing at her jacket with his balled-up white napkin. He shot Mary Alice a menacing look and led the girl toward the restrooms. Mary Alice's lips curled up into a Machiavellian grin.

"Pitiful coat," I said. "It was a public service."

She tossed a hundred-dollar bill on our table and we hurried out.

chapter six

I reread the letter for the hundredth time that evening. Arnie was right. Jennelle was, too. What was the point of inventing silly dramas to put my life on a higher romantic plane? Looks aside, Jordan was another run-of-the-mill adulterer—a member of the twenty-five percent of men who cheated. And with Caroline out of his life—if she was—I wasn't about to become his surrogate lover or dwell on him anymore. I had heard enough stories from friends with married lovers who abandoned them on weekends and holidays. A Saturday evening call with some heavy breathing before the next weekday date was what a woman with a married lover could count on.

Days went by and fortunately Jordan didn't call again. I briefly hit the dating site where Jennelle met Daniel. Sooner or later someone promising had to come along. Then one night as I was about to step into the bath, the phone rang.

"Sage?"

I had a visceral response to his voice. So much for

pretending I had forgotten him.

"Yes."

"I have to talk to you."

"Jordan?"

"Not exactly."

"What are you talking about?"

"Sage, I had to call you because I'm flying back to London tomorrow, and I didn't want to leave you with the wrong impression. Despite what you may think...I'm not a cheating rat."

"You've lost me."

"I'm staying in Jordan's apartment, but...I'm not Jordan. My name is Thomas, Thomas Martin. Jordan's out of town and I'm just a friend."

"Oh," I said, startled. "So you met me for a drink and only now you're confessing that you're an imposter?"

"Well...yes, but as I told you, I was intrigued and couldn't resist."

"So I have yet to meet the real Jordan," I said, the realization dawning on me. For the first time in more than a week, I felt a glimmer of hope. I tested the bath water with my toe.

"Well...that's right," he said, "but there's one more thing I have to tell you."

I took the phone and sat on the side of the tub. The porcelain felt cold and hard under my naked bottom. I bit the corner of my nail aggressively. "What's that?"

"Well...you see, the Jordan you seemed so fascinated with..."

"Yes?"

"Well, it's...Jordan's not a man. She's a woman."

I didn't answer for a second. "*WHAT?*"

"She's a friend of mine and I suppose she was writing a letter to a girlfriend of hers because, you see...she's gay."

Just when I thought the story couldn't get more convoluted, I found out I was pining away for a woman. "Is there anything *else* you have to tell me?" I asked, suddenly aware that I was pumping my foot up and down and my heart was thumping in my chest like a nervous animal caught in a trap.

"No...well, yes," he said. "If things were different...I would have loved seeing you again."

"Thanks, Thomas...for nothing," I said. I started to hang up and then stopped. "Just one more thing," I said. "If you're not Jordan, why was your voice on her answering machine?"

"It wasn't supposed to be," he said. "But when I fiddled with it, I inadvertently erased her message, so I recorded another."

"But you called me back when I left a message for Jordan."

"She was overseas. I thought it might be important."

"So why didn't you say straight out when you called me back that you weren't Jordan?"

"You didn't give me a chance," he said. "You started talking about the love letter I wrote and your feelings and you sounded like such a romantic that, well, I was drawn in."

"Hmmm," *I* said, this time.

"I doubt you'd believe anything I'd say *now*," he said, "but truly, there was nothing nefarious about it."

I nipped at the corner of my nail. "Right."

The only saving grace in the whole embarrassing episode

was knowing that no one except for me and Thomas—who, fortunately, was leaving the country—knew how fate had made a mockery of my life. I had been cast inside the theater of the absurd. I wanted to put it all behind me, forget Jordan, Thomas, the letter, even the taxi ride.

But a nagging thought wouldn't let go of me.

What if I still didn't have the whole story? Why should I believe Thomas, if that was his name? His credibility was still suspect. He lied once, so the seed of doubt was planted. Maybe he really *was* Jordan, but since he was married, he sought to protect himself so he denied it was him to cover his identity. Thomas Martin. Definitely sounded like an alias. Then again, if you wanted to come up with an alias, wouldn't you pick something more out of the ordinary? Martin was as commonplace as Smith, or Jones—it was immediately suspect.

I waited until the weekend and called Jordan's number again. If Jordan really was a she, I needed confirmation from her. I called once and got a machine, but this time the message was one of those disembodied robotic recordings saying the party you were trying to reach wasn't available. Did I even have the right number? I kept calling throughout the weekend, but it was always the machine. I hated the thought of it tallying up all of my hangups, keeping score of my obsessive persistence. Any sane person would assume they were being stalked. I was becoming pathological, yet something kept propelling me to keep on. Then it was Sunday evening at ten. I lifted the receiver once more. If no one answered, that would be it. I'd put it all behind me, never mind that I had more questions than answers.

When you're expecting a machine, it's jarring to hear a

real voice and it takes a moment to process that. "Jordan?" I said, almost startled.

"Yes." Caution in her voice. Who wanted to be phoned at ten on a Sunday night by a stranger? I didn't go into any of the details of the story about the letter. It was too much to lay on a complete stranger.

"I was talking with Thomas Martin," I said. "And he was telling me about you, so I wondered if we could get together and talk, even for a few minutes."

"Why?"

She was now probably assuming that a complete stranger was hitting on her. No wonder she was wary, and annoyed.

"I know it sounds strange…and I hate to bother you, but since we talked, I wanted to tell you about our conversation because it doesn't quite add up." I was bungling things completely, making it worse, not better. Why hadn't I thought this through more carefully?

"Look, I'm really busy," she said, making little attempt to hide her annoyance.

"It wouldn't take long …"

"Give me your number and I'll get back to you."

I gave her my cell, said something lame, and hung up. A complete stranger calling and babbling about her friend Thomas Martin. Why should she care? I was a closet queen, not a trial lawyer, and I'd failed at laying out a convincing case. She'd never call and I'd never get to the bottom of who wrote the letter. Things weren't getting better, they were getting worse.

chapter seven

One way to distance yourself from your own petty obsessions is by helping others. It also boosts your sense of self-worth, they say. I needed mind drainage, so I went online to my volunteer group, where I went through the list of needy spots and I signed up for the children's floor of a major medical center to spend time with kids whose problems dwarfed my own.

The corridors on the pediatric floor were decorated with drawings the children had done. I studied the wall of pictures: Stick-figure children and families in worlds of green grass and deep yellow sun that radiated like spokes on a wheel. There were happy faces, sad ones. Some of the drawings were of the children themselves. One showed tears on the face of a girl with a giant needle sticking out of her arm. A spider was trapped in a web in another. And one showed the word *OOOOWWWW* in bold, black letters running across the top of the page.

I picked up a stack of books near the nurses' station and

walked into a room where I found Laura, her head propped up on two pillows. She sat immobile, staring at the TV over the foot of her bed. I had met her for the first time on my last visit, a month earlier. She was nine or ten and not more than five feet tall, with pale skin and intense blue eyes that beamed out like searchlights. She was so frail and delicate I thought she'd sprout little butterfly wings on the back of her white-and-green hospital gown and take flight.

Her sparse hair was silken. I looked at her slender arms, the translucent white of skimmed milk. But what stayed in my mind most were her feet. Each toe was pencil thin, her bony joints protruding like tiny marbles through her skin. How could her tiny feet bear her weight?

She came to the hospital on a regular schedule for treatments, I found out. In between, she went home and went to school. Even though she looked tired and spent much of the time in bed, her condition didn't seem to diminish her interest in things around her.

"Your blouse is so pretty," she said to me when I entered her room. I had on a fitted tuxedo shirt in pale pink with embroidered ruffles down the front.

"I bought it at a sale," I said, "and I just about got knocked down fighting for it because it was the last one." I acted it out and Laura started to giggle as I poked around wildly into the air with my elbows, getting more theatrical, feeling this frantic need to entertain to fill up the deafening quiet of the room with a voice, silly sounds, life.

"You have such pretty clothes." She examined some gold charms on the zipper pull of my bag. She told me about the blue satin dress she wore for her birthday with the navy-blue velvet sash that tied around her waist. She wore it the day her parents took her to see *The Lion King*.

"And I had a hat," she added. "To cover …" She didn't finish the sentence. "It was dumb looking."

After the show they went to her favorite Italian restaurant for lasagna. But she never had a chance to finish and order ice cream cake. "I got tired," she said, going quiet. "We had to go."

"What's your favorite ice cream flavor?"

"Pistachio."

"Next time I visit, I'll bring you a whole quart." Then I paused. Should I mention a scarf to cover her head? Was that going too far? I reached into my purse. I always carried half a dozen scarves with me, in different colors. They came in handy to brighten jackets or work as shawls. I took them out and put them in front of her.

"Pick your favorite," I said.

Her eyes opened wide. "Really?"

"Really."

She picked a pink-and-red chiffon. "I'll show you three ways to wear it," I said. I tied it around her neck first and took out a mirror. "Oh," she said, "that's so pretty." Then I took it off her neck and wrapped it around her shoulders. "In case you're outside and feeling chilly." I held up the mirror. She looked at herself and nodded. "Or on your head," I said. I wrapped it around her head like a turban and knotted it at the side. "Like this."

She looked at herself in the mirror and nodded knowingly. "I like it," she said. "Better than the hat." Her eyes turned sad.

I swallowed hard. "And next time I come, I'll bring you the ice cream."

Her eyes opened wide. "I'll be back in four weeks," she said, as if it were something to look forward to.

"Deal."

Instead of stories, we looked at magazines. We went through the *Vogue* and *Harper's Bazaar* that I had in my bag. I pointed at pictures and said, "Love or hate?" Then each of us voted.

Over-the-knee boots were "love, love, love." So were cashmere hoodies and Tod's bags. But odd hooded dresses from London rated "eeeeeews," and "barf, hate, hate, hate."

I looked up at Laura with the scarf wrapped so elegantly around her head and I wanted to scoop her up and take her home, just like Harry, so she could have a better life with me, a healthy one. She would be my little doll and I could dress her up, play with her, and take her to school. A little girl who would grow up and have the life she deserved, without cancer. Of course, that was ridiculous.

When it was time to go, I gave her a hug. "See you next time," I whispered. She gave me a thumbs-up. I walked out of the building and stood by the elevator for long, painful minutes before it finally stopped. But I didn't get in. I went back to her room and she looked up, surprised.

"I forgot to give you this," I said, taking a small chain with a dangling gold star off my neck. "It goes with the scarf."

"Oh, Sage," she said.

I closed it around her neck and kissed her on the cheek. "It's a magic star," I said. "Just wish on it, and it'll help you get whatever you want." I turned abruptly and ran out the door.

I took the stairs going down, instead of the elevator, my moist eyes blinding me as I went down floor after floor.

I thought about Laura's parents. Where were they? Why weren't they with her? How could they endure having a child who had to have chemotherapy? Maybe her parents were strong. Or maybe they were just inured to the pain by now. Either way, I didn't think I had the strength to look them in the eyes.

chapter eight

I came back to my empty apartment and Harry. I had to open the door slowly because he waited on the mat behind it so he could listen for the sound of me getting out of the elevator. He usually followed me from room to room, unless we had just come back from the dog park and then he would jump on the couch, all seventy pounds of him crushing down the pillows, before falling into a deep sleep.

I checked my answering machine for messages. Jordan never called, and the story behind the letter remained as elusive as the day I found it.

I spent the week out with clients and tried not to think of LW when I was busy searching the stores for particular styles of clothing or standing in a dressing room offering my take on the fit or style of an outfit. I also tried not to think of Laura too much because it made me feel helpless. I could save a dog from euthanasia. Why couldn't I save a little girl?

I came home with a brown paper bag filled with tandoori chicken and there was no one on the other side of the table to share it with. I switched on CNN, and instead of conversation, I read newspapers and magazines. As I was turning the pages, I came upon an ad for a Montblanc pen, and the idea occurred to me. Why not write *Jordan* a letter? I couldn't do worse. I took out some thick blue note cards and used a fountain pen to write my own plea. I told her about my drink with Thomas. I asked if we could get together for a quick cup of coffee to go over what we had discussed. It wouldn't take long, and as soon as she clarified something he'd said, I wouldn't trouble her again. I apologized for sounding mysterious; it was just too much to put in a letter. I put a stamp on the envelope and dropped it down the narrow glass mail chute in my corridor. It fluttered back and forth in the rectangular space like a confined bird until it swooped down to the mailbox in the lobby.

Two days passed, and then three. I spent the time with clients and got home by six. After I walked Harry, we took the service elevator down to the laundry room. I sorted my clothes, comforted by the simplicity of the task. I sat on a bench in the warm, humid room, lulled by the sound of the machines, mesmerized by the motions of other people's clothes circling clumsily in the dryer, the sleeve of a shirt shaking out here and then entwining itself around a bra or the leg of a pair of jeans, like a snug, happy family of clothes in an embrace.

Of all the homemaking tasks, laundry was the only one I didn't mind. Unless a machine broke down, you knew how much time you had to invest. It was efficient, and then you took home your bounty, a large, warm bag of clean, fresh-smelling clothes. Predictable, no risk, no big commitment, no decisions—other than Tide or All. And because most of the people in the building had their housekeepers do their laundry during the day, at night the basement room was a windowless island of calm, a laundry spa where you were spared of outside noises, an isolation tank, as it were. Harry liked to get up on the wooden bench in front of the dryers and watch the laundry getting tossed in circles, too.

After I folded everything, I carried it upstairs. Lulled by the calm of the past hour, I was ready to sleep. But just as I was putting everything away, the phone rang.

"Sage?"

I knew who it was instantly. "Thanks for calling, Jordan." I didn't have time to get nervous this time. We agreed to meet the next morning in the Village, at a Starbucks.

"How will I know you?"

"Short, dark hair," she said. "I'll be wearing a green quilted jacket."

• • •

I got off the subway at Bleecker Street and walked west toward Broadway, where boutiques sell the hottest brands of jeans and the latest Pumas and Nikes in addition to vintage clothes. I passed street vendors selling T-shirts, sunglasses, funky jewelry, and incense, a scene that never seems to change.

Starbucks was crowded, a comforting sign as always, signifying that no matter what issues the world was facing, there was a little haven of normalcy you could go to, a place where people congregated for nothing more than good coffee and the company of people they considered a notch above the rest because they appreciated it. It was worth the stop, even an outing. Sometimes I sat in Starbucks studying what people had on. There were those who planned their outfits and took care that everything went together, and others who dressed with no thought to how the pieces added up.

I headed past the long line at the counter to the back seating area filled with an odd assortment of thick club chairs and wine-colored velvet loveseats. Almost every seat was taken. Mothers with double-size strollers sat among college kids, poetic types on laptops who wanted to get away from their kitchen tables, and fatigued shoppers fueling up on rich cake. I immediately spotted the loden-green, quilted Burberry jacket because of the tan plaid lining peeking out at the cuffs. She was sitting at a small round table, intently reading the *New Yorker*.

"Jordan?" She looked up, almost surprised. "I'm Sage." I pulled out the chair next to her. She tilted her head to the side as if she were assessing me. After taking a sip of coffee, she studied me over the rim. "So?"

A stranger asked to talk with her, cutting into her Saturday. Why wouldn't she plunge in without the formalities? I slipped off my coat, admiring the Burberry bag she placed on the table. Her style was classic. Blunt-cut hair, clear skin without a trace of makeup. No jewelry. Penetrating, intelligent brown eyes. I wondered for a moment whether she had gone to the trouble of calling Thomas to ask who I was.

Trying to be as brief as possible, I went over how I found the letter and how taken I was with the writer. "I know this sounds ridiculous." I raked a hand through my hair, "but from your name, I just assumed you were a man—"

"Everyone does," she said, dismissively.

"Anyway, the letter was so well written, so moving, so… well…compelling, that I became very taken with the person who wrote it. I held out a hand in a helpless gesture. "I hope you don't think I'm completely crazy." She looked amused. "It was just one of those things I had to pursue. So I did some detective work and found your phone number and eventually I reached Thomas."

"He's an old friend from years back. We have this reciprocal thing with our apartments. Both of us prefer to avoid hotels, we hate to eat out alone in restaurants when we travel, we both have guest rooms, so…" She shrugged.

"Anyway, at this point I just wanted to make sure his story was correct," I said, "because when I met him he told me *his* name was Jordan."

She raised an eyebrow. "Really? He's a rogue; I'll have to get after him then."

"So if you *are* the letter writer…then my research is over."

She took another sip of coffee and smiled. It transformed her face from cool and dispassionate to warm and engaging.

"It *was* my letter," she said tentatively, toying with the strap of her bag. "And I was having a relationship with someone named Caroline…but that's not the whole story."

I looked at her questioningly.

"The truth is that I can't really take credit for writing it."

"I don't understand."

"I wrote the letter over and over at first," she said, looking off as though she were remembering. "But I'm such an awful writer—every word sounded so straitlaced, like it came out of a business text. So I leaned on—" she paused, "a friend to help." I waited for her to continue. "Actually it ended up more *his* letter. He suggested the paper and the ink too, and…I basically stole his words."

"Who is *he?*"

"Oh," she said waving her hand to the side. "Luke."

"Last name?"

"Edmond."

"What does he do?" I didn't enjoy playing twenty questions.

"He's an artist."

And let me guess: he's married with four kids…and he lives outside the country…but it was really his second cousin from Tanzania who wrote the letter with the help of his ex-wife who turned to a poet, who unfortunately passed away, but not before…

"I see."

"We were both at RISD."

"Oh." RISD—the Rhode Island School of Design.

"For years I thought I would become a professional illustrator, but then I changed gears completely and started working for Burberry."

That explained the jacket and bag. If I got chummy with her, maybe my clients could get a discount. "How's that going?" I asked, to give the impression that I was not totally one-dimensional.

"It's a good place for me right now, but I like to reinvent myself every few years, so I'm sure I'll be moving on."

"And your friend…Luke…does he live in New York too?"

"He used to, but he wanted to get out of the city—he needed more room for his painting and it's impossible to find affordable studio space here."

"Where did he move?" I was using up more of my questions.

"The last time I spoke to him he was somewhere out on the island."

Long Island? I hoped he wasn't somewhere near the Bermuda triangle. I waited for more specifics. I didn't enjoy peppering her with questions like the DA. She smiled back at me enigmatically. "What do *you* do?"

I told her.

"Well, if you're interested in Burberry stuff," she patted her bag, "call me."

"Thanks. I noticed you looked well put together." Hoping that she wouldn't take that as any more than it was, I pointed to the bag. "Fabulous. It caught my eye the moment it came out."

"Yours and everyone else's." She shook her head. "I think the knockoffs of it have already been knocked off." She drained the last bit of coffee and stood, slipping the bag over her arm. "Well, I've got an appointment with my trainer."

I stood at the same time. "Do you have a number for Luke?" I tried to make it sound like an afterthought.

"He moves around so much, I don't actually know where he's camping out now." She reached into her bag and took out her phone. I waited while she scrolled through her numbers. She held it out to me, finally. "Try this one." I jotted it down on the corner of a coffee-stained napkin. She studied me as if she were sizing me up, not sure what to conclude. I decided right then I wouldn't want her for an enemy.

"Good luck," she said. A moment later she turned and waved. I watched her make her way out through the crowd. Then I remembered. I had forgotten to ask her about Caroline.

chapter nine

Another piece to the puzzle and now, instead of dwelling on Jordan, it was Luke. The name was good, that was a start. Perhaps it was no coincidence that Saint Luke was supposed to have written the third Gospel and the Acts of the Apostles. Only this Luke was an artist. I looked him up on the net. Only a few scattered references to group shows in the Village. No listing of a gallery affiliation. No website. No pictures of his work. Or of him. Basically, he was invisible.

I planned to meet Jennelle and Daniel for dinner at a small Asian restaurant uptown. Jennelle and I would make informed choices—steamed shrimp, scallop dumplings, maybe Vietnamese shrimp rolls. Daniel, a raging carnivore, would seize on a giant slab of something life-threatening.

I should have been mature enough to have kept the whole letter business to myself. But no, I rushed to tell Jennelle, who was equally immature and immediately shared it with Daniel. No doubt it would become the focus of dinner conversation. After ordering, Daniel looked up at me expectantly.

One, two, three…

"So, Sage, did you talk to the dude?"

I shot Jennelle a withering look. She found it amusing. I dipped a spring roll into soy sauce, lifting it to my mouth, but not fast enough to avoid leaving a trail of splattered brown dots on the white tablecloth so it resembled a Japanese watercolor. "Not yet."

"Why *not?*" she said.

"I've been swamped."

She lifted an eyebrow. I took another bite and pretended to be concentrating on the food. Why *didn't* I call him? I had worked hard to get the number and now it was sitting at home on my bureau. It had something to do with savoring the idea that the ball was in my court, giving me time to decide how to play it. Waiting meant I was alive. Once I met him and became disillusioned, it was over. And chances were that's what would happen. The whole encounter would be a crushing disappointment. Luke would be a big, clumsy, stupid man, nothing like the creative, romantic figure my imagination gave life to based on nothing more than a letter expressing someone else's sentiments. He might be a tour de force with a pen, but a disaster in real life.

Since Daniel was in the art supply business, there was a chance he might know Luke.

"I'll have to check with the guys in the store who do the day-to-day stuff," he said. "But the name doesn't sound familiar."

The way things were going, it wouldn't have surprised me if Luke didn't even exist. Jordan might be playing me, or making a film with Thomas, who was making it with

Greg. They were all out to hoodwink me for the cinematic possibilities. I wasn't getting too paranoid. What I did find out was that Daniel had a show of his own painting coming up during Christmas week. They had ads up in the store, he said. Guaranteed, it would draw lots of artists.

"You have to come," Jennelle said. "If you don't hit it off with Luke, you can meet someone else." She gave Daniel a strange look. "I might."

Trouble in paradise? If there was, it wasn't something that she had shared with me—yet.

Daniel raised his eyebrows. "Stop."

"I wouldn't miss it," I said, ignoring whatever it was between them. Parties and openings were like fashion shows for me. Fads came as much from what designers saw on the streets as from new takes on styles of the past. Wedged into the frame of my bedroom mirror was a quote from Chanel: "Fashion is not something that exists in dresses only; fashion is something in the air. It's the wind that blows in the new fashion; you feel it coming, you smell it…in the sky, in the street; fashion has to do with ideas, the way we live, what is happening."

I studied Jennelle's outfit. It was perfect on her. A vintage black leather Alaia jacket with a nipped waist, and under it, a scarlet T-shirt and tight jeans with high-heeled boots. We bought everything she had on one day when we were shopping along Broadway and down in Soho. She had her own style now, and she dressed with confidence and ease. Wear your old clothes like they're new, and new clothes like they're old, the French said.

"So I have news." She shimmied her shoulders. "My workdays of dull business suits and sensible pumps are over."

"Citibank is closing down? The CEO is being indicted?"

"Nooo, I've given notice at work. I'm going to rep a group of artists."

In some small way, I thanked myself for giving her a ticket over the wall. Jennelle had bitched about her job for years, but she'd never had the nerve to resign. Despite regular paychecks and health benefits, the bank was a pit. I was convinced that her new image (it had only been about a year) helped her get a creative leg up.

I hoisted my fist into the air. "Yes!"

"The ad agencies are always looking for new artists," Daniel said. "If Jennelle can represent a good group of people, after some initial pavement pounding it could turn into a decent living."

He leaned over and put his arm around her, nuzzling her neck. She had a look in her eyes I didn't recognize. I always thought of Daniel as more than a boyfriend. They were like partners, building their lives together, while Greg and I went down separate career paths. To him, I had a job and he had an obsession. I don't think he gave a second thought to what I did when I was away from him for ten hours a day. On good days I saw the magic in it, but he saw only the drudgery. He didn't get the connection between clothes and the psyche, and never would.

They dropped me at my apartment after dinner. As I opened the door, part of me still expected to see Greg stretched out on the couch, watching a movie made by some world-acclaimed director, and calling out to me to come watch some iconic movie moment. I'd sit down and watch, rarely sharing his passion. When the DVD player wasn't on, he'd be reading something out loud to me, like an article describing Kurosawa's attempted suicide following an unproductive five-year spell topped off by the release of a movie (*Dodes'ka-den*) that was a box-office bomb. I guess it gave him hope that Kurosawa's next film, *Dersu Uzala*, won an Oscar in 1975 for best foreign film and a gold medal at the Moscow Film Festival.

I flipped on the TV to the local news on channel one. Harry joined me in bed, rolling onto his back so I could scratch his stomach. If I stopped too soon, he shook his paw up and down as if he were pointing to his stomach. At least *we* understood each other.

chapter ten

I went to the supermarket and bought the fanciest quart of pistachio ice cream I could find. I packed it up with ice and made my way to the hospital. Laura had another treatment and I wasn't sure what kind of shape she'd be in. Chemo exhausted you, but I hoped at least she'd have an appetite for ice cream, since she needed the calories so badly.

She was sleeping when I arrived. I stood by her bed, watching her, the sound of a kid's movie of some sort playing in the background. Her calm, angelic face was perfectly proportioned. She looked as if she were chiseled out of fine white marble by a Renaissance sculptor. Bow-shaped lips, a small, straight nose, and perfect skin setting off her large, deep-set eyes. I sat in the chair facing her bed and decided to wait, rather than waking her. I was checking my phone for messages when she opened her eyes.

"Sage?"

"How are you feeling?"

"Sleepy, but okay," she said. I held out the bag and

pulled out the quart of ice cream. "Ta-da!"

"You remembered!" Laura dug the plastic spoon I gave her into the quart and began to eat. I glanced down at the star necklace around her neck, and looked away. She licked the first spoonful clean and rolled her eyes. She took another, then another. And then she stopped and put the spoon down. Her eyelids fluttered from exhaustion. I pretended not to understand.

"I'm still full from dinner," she said. I didn't ask her what was for dinner. I guessed it was soup and maybe a few bites of hamburger. That was probably all she could tolerate. My subterfuge, as usual, was distraction.

"Want to watch some television?"

She nodded and I grabbed the remote and channel-surfed. We came to the home shopping channel. They were selling cheap, ugly dresses. I stuck my tongue out and Laura giggled. "Haute couture," I sniffed. I pretended to be fascinated and Laura pretended too, but I saw her eyes closing.

"Maybe I should go and let you catch up on sleep," I whispered. She opened her eyes and nodded.

"I'll see you soon, pumpkin," I said. As I walked out, I saw the scarf. It was draped over the chair, nearby.

As I went to bed that night, I thought of the ice cream sitting near her bed, slowly melting.

• • •

The tan napkin with the French roast Rorschach stain and the phone number in black marker was tucked under a red leather jewelry box on my bureau. Half of the number peeped out—*631-32*—like the edge of the envelope, a reminder of someone else's life whenever I opened my drawer for lingerie.

I collected lingerie the way other people collected stamps, coins, or rare porcelain. I had a dreamy collection of silks, voiles, crocheted cottons—things I found wherever I traveled. Did it matter that no one would see me in the yellow chiffon demi bra with the satin ribbon trim, the sea-green silk thong, or the lavender silk nightgown?

"Buy it for yourself, because it makes *you* feel good," I told clients. Their private pleasures would enhance how they presented themselves to the world. I had to remind myself of that.

Two weeks had passed. The letter was written months before, I imagined. He had probably forgotten it by now. What could be more bizarre than a stranger phoning and asking to meet you because you helped a friend write a letter?

But then, why not? It was a *love* letter, a romantic throwback to the past. Why not satisfy my curiosity? I dialed the number, staring out the window as it rang. Once, twice, three times, four, five, and I hung up. Not home. It was now out of my hands. Then I pressed redial. I waited through another impossibly long set of rings. I was relieved. I wasn't looking forward to another strange encounter. So I went on with my life and the napkin remained tucked under the jewelry box.

About a week later, after I had finished dinner and decided after one glass of wine that I'd finish off the bottle, I tried again. Only this time it didn't ring and ring.

"The number you have dialed has been disconnected…"

Was Jordan aware that Luke's number was disconnected?

Had he moved? I called information.

"No listing for that name," she said.

Now what? I didn't relish calling Jordan again. I felt like I was becoming a stalker, but what else could I do? She was as elusive as Luke. I tried her several times and always got the machine. For someone with a regular job, she didn't seem to be at home on a steady basis, unless she was the type to screen her calls. Would I have better luck reaching her at Burberry?

I waited until eleven thirty the next day. Late enough for people who drifted in late, and early enough to be sure she wasn't already out for lunch. Bingo, she answered her phone.

"I tried your number for Luke," I said. "It was disconnected."

She groaned. "He probably couldn't pay his phone bill."

I waited, curious to hear what she'd suggest.

"All I can say is your best bet is to go see him, if you can find him."

"Where does he live?"

"Out on Long Island. Got a pen?"

I scrawled down the address. "You just fall in on him?"

"You can try. Luke's like a fast-moving target who camouflages himself in the brush," she said with a laugh. "He goes and comes and you're never sure when there will be a sighting."

"Maybe I should bring fresh meat," I said. "I can smoke him out with the scent."

"Now there's an idea. He's usually starving."

I tucked the address into my wallet and thanked her again. If this didn't work, the only thing I could think of was to put Harry on his trail.

• • •

"I think Daniel's having an affair."

Jennelle didn't sound crushed; it was more reportorial. She got up from the table abruptly and went to a closet on the wall for a second bottle of Chardonnay.

"Based on what?"

"On nothing—or almost nothing." She searched for the corkscrew. It was right in front of her. "Just instinct."

"Is he less interested in sex?"

"Just the opposite." She filled her glass and reached for another piece of Kentucky Fried Chicken. Were we indulging ourselves or punishing ourselves? I hadn't decided which. "It's as if he feels guilty and wants to make up for it."

"When did things change?"

"He came home from the store late one night."

"And?"

She put down the chicken leg. "I don't know," she said, as if she were mulling it over. "It was just something about the way he looked. The way his eyes shone."

Would I notice something like that? Just before Greg left me for that Bohemian bitch actress with the trashy East Village look, our sex life was almost nonexistent. I thought he had Epstein–Barr.

"And that was *it*, just the look of his eyes?"

"Yeah."

"Did you ask him where he was?"

"He said he was out for a drink with a buddy, but he doesn't do much of that."

"I don't think you have a strong case."

"It's just that I know Daniel," she said. "And now there's

this mystery between us."

"Would it be the end of the world if you found out he was with somebody?"

"He's a terrible liar," she said. She stared into her wine as though it were a crystal ball. "And what gets me most is he won't admit it."

"Would you?"

She gave me an annoyed look.

"Take a step back," I said. "If he was cheating on you, he'd want you to keep your job at the bank, wouldn't he? Why would he want you to represent the artists who come into his store and know all about his life?"

"Life isn't always logical," Jennelle said. "Things just happen."

"Or you make them happen," I said.

chapter eleven

How long does it take to make a first impression?

Three seconds.

About the same time it takes to snap your picture. The impression you give someone in those few seconds becomes fixed in their minds, as indelible as a photograph. So a woman who's going on a job interview has to enter the workplace in an outfit that makes her look well groomed and professional—and that's not something that just happens. It takes planning. Only thousands of women who need jobs and are faced with job interviews don't have the money to buy a suit, a bag, shoes, and stockings to dress for success. And some of them wouldn't even know where to begin if they did.

So one weekday, instead of the hospital where I met Laura, or the city dog shelter, I offered to help a national organization called Success in Dress, whose mission is to give women the clothes they need to get new jobs and improve their lives.

That's where I met Gretchen Harrison. Gretchen needed a new life and the clothes to wear for a job to support it. Five years before, she couldn't have imagined herself in a brand-new suit heading for an interview for a job as a clerk in a real estate office. She was trapped in a loveless relationship with an abusive husband who beat her. But with no income of her own other than welfare money, moving out didn't seem to be an option. Then there were her five children to care for.

But one day, after she spent the afternoon at the local emergency room because a gash on her face needed twenty stitches, Gretchen looked at herself in a mirror in the hospital.

"That was it," she told me. "I had enough. I had less than thirty dollars in my pocket, but I took my kids and we found a room at a city shelter for women like me." She looked off in the distance as if she were reliving it. "Battered women," she whispered.

They got her children enrolled in a new school and helped Gretchen take a course where she learned to use a computer. Within weeks of graduating, she heard about a job at a local real estate company. But since she had never worked and had no money to shop, she needed clothes to wear to the interview.

At the offices of Success in Dress, I helped her find a suit from the large inventory they had from not only donations of gently used clothes but also new clothes donated by stores or bought with money from outside supporters.

We found a navy-blue pinstripe suit, size fourteen. It fit her perfectly. I picked out a pale blue blouse that she wore under it, along with black pumps and a black shoulder bag.

I tied a blue patterned scarf on the handle of the bag for a dash of flair. She put on the outfit and stared at herself in the three-way mirror.

"I never wore a suit before," she said, shaking her head as she studied herself in a three-way mirror. "Or owned a real leather purse."

"How do you feel?" I said.

She threw back her head and laughed. A moment later, she broke into tears.

• • •

Under the list of dos and don'ts for job seekers, Success in Dress advises women to tell themselves that they deserve the job. I looked at Gretchen and wondered whether she could look in the mirror on the morning of the interview and believe that. Women from abusive homes weren't used to reciting mantras about self-worth. They might have started out in life with self-esteem, but more often than not it was beaten out of them.

A week after Gretchen's job interview, she called and told me she got the job. She hooted with delight. The company made her feel they accepted her, and believed in her, she said.

"Those people made me feel like my life has value," Gretchen said. "And no matter what happens," she said, "I'm going to always keep the suit I wore to the interview." She called it her "lucky suit."

In addition to the navy-blue suit, Success in Dress gave her enough clothes for a week's worth of outfits. Getting a job turned her into a different woman.

But it had less to do with the fact that she cut her hair short in a flattering style. Or that looking good motivated her to walk more so that she could lose weight and look trimmer. It had a lot to do with self-worth. At the end of the day, she came home knowing she helped things run smoothly for an office full of people who depended on her. People who smiled and said good morning. Or brought in cookies they left for her in a napkin on her desk. It had everything to do with a feeling she never had when she lived with an abusive husband, and all she felt was hate and fear. Her five children were learning about that new feeling too.

It was called love.

chapter twelve

My newest client was a man who lived in the Village. Men usually came with less baggage, and more often than not, they freely took your advice—sometimes slavishly—when you went shopping with them. The hardest clients were the men whose wives or girlfriends tagged along so there were two personalities to deal with, not to mention the tension between what she thought he should buy and what I did. On top of that, there was the inherent resentment women harbored when other women told their man what he needed. Then there were the wives who didn't want their spouses looking all that good. I was a definite threat to the security of those types and they vetoed my selections altogether. After enduring a few tense sessions, I made a hard and fast rule: shopping was a one-on-one activity.

Brian Schulberg lived on University Place in a prewar building that was a smart residential hotel before it was converted into an apartment building. It was on the northeast corner of Washington Square Park, just down the street from the arch designed by Stanford White to commemorate the centennial of Washington's inauguration as president. The doorman announced me and I went up to the twentieth floor. Brian's apartment had an expansive view of the park, but the furnishings were sparse.

I glanced around. "Did you just move in?"

He shook his head. "Nah, I've been here for two hours."

I liked clients who made me laugh. We had fun together and worked more productively than if I had to endure the company of someone troubled and depressed. Brian's apartment had what he needed—a leather couch, two club chairs, and an L-shaped desk in the corner that held various computers and components. There were file cabinets along the wall. I assumed that there was a bedroom with a bed. Now he needed a wardrobe.

In short, he dressed to keep himself from getting arrested. Overall the effect was dorky, but it didn't have to be. Brian was middle-aged, about five foot eight with dark, slightly thinning hair. Good skin (obviously not the outdoors type), and with a slight paunch. The haircut was awful. So were the dated glasses along with the short-sleeve, wash-and-wear shirt, the ill-fitting chinos, and unattractive loafers.

Statistics show that fifty-three percent of men spend less than two minutes each day picking out their clothes. Brian was one of them, unless the whole thing was a setup. Would my friends come out of the bedroom yelling, "HAPPY BIRTHDAY!"? Chances are they wouldn't, and not just because my birthday was two months away. Still, this guy was peculiar. Why did he decide to suddenly get help?

The way I usually began was by sitting down and talking about why someone had called me and what they hoped to accomplish—a kind of nonconfrontational, "how can I help you" approach, rather than "So I see that you need a makeover," or "I imagine that you want a wardrobe that makes you look thinner." I learned that from a friend who was a plastic surgeon. His opening line was always something benign, like, "Why have you come to see me?"

With women, I sometimes started as much as a few weeks before by sending them a client intake form asking questions like: What's your favorite color, movie, book, vacation destination, actor, actress, car, etc. What's your best time of day, what are your goals? I sometimes asked them to cut out magazine pictures they liked of all types of outfits and living styles. The pictures showed not only clothes on models but also homes, accessories, colors, gardens, or just about anything that appealed to them, which gave me snapshots of their taste and style.

Men rarely had the patience or interest in activities like that, so I started with some basic questions about their jobs and their lifestyles. Brian told me that he had recently gone through a divorce, and had now met a woman online. They were going to see each other for the first time and he wanted to make a good impression. I held my tongue. *Are you sure she's a she? Are you sure she didn't send you a picture of Heidi Klum?*

He was no wide-eyed boy, though, and it was unfair to be cynical. My heart went out to him, actually. He wasn't exactly hot, and he was nervous. He wanted to make a good impression and he wanted it to go right. Like all of us, he simply wanted to fall in love.

"What do you do for a living?"

"Computer software."

"Do you work in an office?"

He pointed to the computer. "I'm here most of the time. I'm on my own."

No top-tier zeitgeist. "What kind of clothes do you usually wear on the job and off?"

"Whatever I want," he said. He gestured toward what he had on. "Like this."

"And what kind of look are you aiming for?" I could tell he didn't know how to answer.

"How do you see me?"

"As someone who's pretty casual. But I think you need clothes that are higher quality and look more sophisticated. More of a monochromatic look that will flatter your body and coloring."

He nodded, obviously willing to go along. "Our date is tomorrow night," he said, as if it were a minor detail. "So we have to get going."

I looked at him questioningly and shook my head in disbelief. "Tomorrow night?"

"Right, we're having dinner."

"Brian, it doesn't work that way. I usually spend a few days with a client over the course of a few weeks. We go through what you have, decide what you need, go shopping. The process can take some time."

"I don't have time," he said, matter-of-factly, as if he didn't hear me. "I have to have the clothes by tomorrow night at eight."

"I don't even have tomorrow free. I've got two—"

"Look, whatever it is, I'll make it worth your while," he said. "I'll pay you ten times whatever you'd get for tomorrow's clients. How's that?"

I looked back at him and didn't say anything. "It's that

important," I said, as a statement, rather than a question.

"Definitely."

I looked at my watch. "Well then, let's jump into a cab and go up to Barneys right now. Why leave it for the last minute?"

At least he was easy to shop for. He followed me around like a compliant puppy, never complaining when I sent him into the dressing room, nearly felled by a yard-high stack of clothes to try. He reminded me of another male client who said to me, "Just pretend I'm a paper doll and dress me."

After he suggested a few items of clothes that I rejected with a silent shake of my head, he resigned himself to whatever I picked out. A quick study, he eventually detected the differences between the fabrics, hues, and styles that flattered him, and the ones that didn't. Brian was the type of guy who lived in washable khaki pants, so it amused him to hear that they originated in India during Queen Victoria's reign when a British officer thought of dyeing white uniforms with a mix of curry powder and coffee as a way of hiding stains. In Brian's case, even the khaki coloration didn't help.

We picked out replacement khakis that looked and fit better than his, and then moved to lightweight gabardine trousers. Canali jackets were next, and then shirts—a few with French cuffs, because they peek out of a jacket and make your arms look longer. We rounded up Armani ties (they should hit the top of your belt buckle), a few Armani cashmere sweaters, long cashmere socks (leave the short ones to Italian bus drivers), shoes by Tod's and Ferragamo, and a great Hermès watch.

As Michael Kors advised: "If you're not great-looking,

wear a fabulous watch, carry expensive luggage, and wear sunglasses. It worked for Onassis."

To my relief, Brian didn't care about prices. I made a haircut appointment for him the next day, with notes to the hairdresser, who was a friend of mine. The only thing we couldn't fix in time were the glasses. I was half tempted to leave them once we took him up several notches in his choice of clothes, a kind of reverse chic accessory that would stand out. I wrote down the name of a store where he could get fitted for new frames and told him to pick out rectangular tortoiseshell frames. His face was oval and the shape of the glasses needed to contrast. If I didn't trust the saleswoman in the store whom I knew, I would have agreed to go with him.

By the time Barneys closed, Brian had a week's worth of outfits. The two of us were hauling out so many bags that we looked as though we had just stepped off a plane with our luggage. When we got back to his apartment, he ordered pizza from Patsy's up the street, and while we waited I put all the outfits together and took pictures of what went with what. I also gave him a lesson in properly hanging clothes and how to care for them.

"Nothing goes back to your closet if it needs cleaning, or tailoring, and never press clothes without cleaning them if you don't absolutely have to. It seals in the dirt." Everything hanging up in your closet should be ready to wear, I said. We finished at ten and I was ready to drop.

"Before you go, what should I wear to meet her?" he said. "What's my best look?"

I pulled out a tan shirt with an Armani tie and a slightly darker patterned jacket, along with chocolate-brown gabardine pants and Ferragamo loafers. Brian went into the bedroom and changed into it and looked at me. I saw that vulnerability that so many clients have shown me when they put on clothes they'd never worn before.

"We nailed it," I said. "You look great."

He studied himself in the mirror on the back of the closet door. "Yeah," he said finally, pressing his lips together, getting into the new look. He seemed to grow taller and more commanding before my eyes. "It feels good, yeah."

He paraded around the apartment with head held high, as if he were rehearsing for what was ahead.

"Promise me you'll let me know how things go."

"I will," he said. "Thank you. Really, Sage."

I put my arms around him and hugged him.

One of the most gratifying and yet disturbing things about my work was that I was there for people in the vast field of new beginnings—before taking on new jobs, going off on trips, starting relationships, and all kinds of fresh starts. I was like a life coach who helped people live better lives. On the other hand, after hundreds or thousands of dollars of the other person's money was spent, if I'd done my job right, they could dress without me. In those cases, I stepped aside and it was often bittersweet to think about how they'd fare as they went off on their own. While some clients called me back season after season, others were like graduates who left with their caps and gowns, ready to start the next phase of their lives, leaving me behind to search for new clients to help, wondering whatever happened to the Brian Schulbergs of the world.

So I left his apartment with the biggest check I had ever earned for one day of work. I came home and sat down in front of the computer. I was curious to find out about Brian. I sensed that there was more to this enigmatic man than he had revealed on our whirlwind shopping day. I went through listings on Google and MSN, and it didn't take long to find out.

His small software company was bought by Microsoft in 2001. Despite his no-frills apartment and schlumpy clothes, Brian Schulberg was a billionaire who obviously had everything—except what money couldn't buy.

chapter thirteen

When I wasn't volunteering or trying to better someone else's life, I'd come home and think about my long-term prospects. One of them was still the letter. The more time that passed, the more absurd it looked—making a day trip out of the city to confront a stranger. But it happened to be the weekend, and the weather was on my side. Late October, a brilliant fall day, and winter still a way off. It would be invigorating to be out on Long Island in farm country, passing stands that sold apples, squash, and pumpkins. Fall foliage was in color and this would be a chance to see the leaves. Every year when the newspaper mapped the best routes, I always considered driving north but I never did. I was waiting for the right person to go with me.

I wouldn't be far from Mary Alice. I could visit. Her wardrobe had grown like kudzu, now filling her closet and the empty one that had been her husband's. Reconciliation didn't look like an option. She sent me emails about her wearying trips to the city to negotiate divorce terms with her lawyer.

So there I was in a rented Honda Accord in the parking lot of a deli in East Quogue, eating a decent tuna salad sandwich with lettuce and tomato on whole wheat. Just enough mayo, a little bit of sweet green relish. My Arizona peach iced tea was balanced between my knees. I didn't drive for two and a half hours for the tuna, though.

I drove there because I hoped that although Luke Edmond didn't have a phone he'd be home and answer his door.

Once I got off the highway, I continued along small rutted roads that could have been lifted out of the rolling plains of the Midwest. I was only a couple of hours outside the city, but this was a sparsely populated area with few cars around—farm country that off-season is blue collar, not no collar. From a map that the attendant at the gas station made for me, it looked as though Luke's house was a couple of miles down a small dirt road. I passed a farm with an APPLES FOR SALE sign, and bought a bag.

The road curved past small, isolated houses and I followed it until I came to a two-story white wooden New England–style farmhouse with a small front porch that had two red wooden rockers on it. It sat on an open expanse of land with tall trees on the perimeter. There were no other houses around it. No one seemed to be around.

The house looked like it was lifted from a stage set for *Our Town*. I saw a beat-up black pickup truck when I went around to the side of the house. I walked up the creaky steps to the front door and knocked. No answer. I knocked again and then rang the bell. I peered through the window. No sign of movement or anyone around. It was dark inside. I could barely make out a striped sofa and a couple of thick club chairs. Hard to imagine this was just a few miles from multimillion-dollar Hamptons weekend homes. This house was what would be politely described as a tear-downer.

I gave up and walked around to the back, hoping a giant pit bull wouldn't charge out and clamp me in its jaws. There was a separate building in the back that looked like it had once been a barn. Now there were large sliding doors and big windows on two sides. I walked over and looked inside. Almost empty except for a row of paintings propped up against a wall and a long industrial table with metal boxes on top of it. I stared at one painting in particular. It was done in vibrant blues, greens, and purples. I thought of leaving a note, but if he was never there to answer the phone, why would he be there to see the note?

I was about to get back into the car when I looked off into the distance. The sun was in my eyes, and I wasn't certain, but it looked like someone was out in the field behind the house. I walked back there and realized there was a figure in front of something large and rectangular. I got closer and saw that it was a canvas. I thought about calling out to him to let him know I was there before I moved in on him. When I was about fifteen feet away, I stopped.

"Hello…excuse me, are you Luke?" There was a silence for a few seconds.

"Luke who?" he said finally, without turning.

"Edmond?"

"Does he owe you money?"

"No."

"Then I'm Luke Edmond."

He turned and looked at me inquiringly for a few brief seconds before he went back to his canvas, as if that settled that. I studied him as quickly as he studied me. Straight blond, streaked hair, razor cut, parted on the side. It fell in two long sections, each ending at the edge of his unshaven jaw. The back was a few inches longer. A pierced ear with a small gold hoop earring. Tanned skin, light green eyes. Despite the chill, all he had on was a denim shirt over jeans. He was barefoot.

I stood, watching him, assuming he had to finish a particular section and after he did he'd turn back to me to find out why I was there. But no, he seemed to block me out entirely. Finally, annoyed, I walked closer.

"Aren't you going to ask why I'm here?" I was unable to hide the trace of annoyance in my voice.

"Nope."

"I'll tell you why," I said, ignoring his answer, "and then I'll get into my car and you can keep on painting." He turned around for a second glance before turning back to the canvas.

"I found a letter that you wrote—actually, the letter that you wrote for your friend Jordan. I found it in a taxi. And, well, even though now I find it hard to believe…you did a really fine job of writing it. I mean, who ever writes love letters these days? And so here I am. I tracked you down." My outburst was followed by another long, irritating pause.

"So now what?" he said, finally.

"*Now what?*" I repeated in a low, controlled voice. I had gone to the trouble of taking off an entire day, standing in line for half an hour to rent a car at Avis, driving two and a half hours by myself out to Nowheresville, Long Island, to track down an artist who wrote a letter that made me swoon, only to find out he had an annoying attitude, that in real life he clearly preferred silence to speech, and now he was completely cold to the entire story, not to mention me.

"Now I'm getting back into my car and driving the whole way back to Manhattan. Goodbye, and I truly hope we never meet again."

With that, he turned around and stared. "You are some little piece of work," he said, with the barest hint of a smile. He looked me over and his eyes fixed on my boots. Then his whole expression changed. He got off the stool and walked closer, then stopped, studying them. Finally, he knelt at my feet, pulling up the leg of my jeans.

"Hey, what do—"

He whistled softly. "Where did you get these?"

I had several pairs of cowboy boots, but these were my favorite. They were decorated with flowers and vintage guns. I hate guns, but I loved the way they looked on the boots.

"Santa Fe. I had them made. You like them?"

He didn't answer and shook his head in disbelief. "Take them off."

"Why?" I shook my head, uncertainly.

He didn't answer again, as he stared, running his fingers along the colored stitching. Finally, I sat down and tugged one off, and then the other, and he took them and turned them over, studying the soles, the heels, and the design on the leather. He put one down on the ground, then the other, and looked at them. Finally, he stood.

"Can I borrow them?"

"What?"

He repeated the question patiently.

"I can't go home barefoot."

"Why not?"

"Because it's fifty degrees, and I live in the middle of Manhattan."

He nodded. "Can you send them to me, then?"

"What are you going to do with them?" I asked, like a nervous parent who is asked to lend her child to someone.

"Paint them," he said, as though it should have been obvious.

"I don't think so. They cost me a fortune."

No reaction as he stared back at me and fixed his eyes on the boots again. He shrugged and turned, walking back toward the house. Something about his gait struck me as odd. It was slow and deliberate. I thought he was pretending at first, and then I saw that he wasn't. He walked with his head down so that his hair fell forward, almost hiding his face. I followed him, heading to my car.

He stopped at the front door of his house and leaned his arm up against the door. "Goodbye, Miss Cowboy Boots."

I met his eyes for a long minute, then squeezed mine shut. "Okay, I'll send them…if you promise to send them back."

"I will," he said, holding my gaze.

I got into my car and stuck my arm out to wave goodbye. As I turned on the motor, he held up his hand to stop me. He came over and leaned into the window. Then I realized why his gait was strange. He had a limp.

"It's not that I'm unsociable or anything," he said, softly. "It's just that I don't have any…well…anything at all to eat or drink in the house, so…" He didn't finish the sentence. His awkwardness was like a moat around him.

"What are *you* going to eat?"

He shrugged. "I'm not. No money until tomorrow or the next day."

I reached into the back seat for the bag of apples and handed it to him through the window. "Here, I wouldn't want you to starve." He took the bag with a shy smile, then walked back toward the house.

chapter fourteen

The small gallery on Greene Street in Soho where Daniel had his show specialized in showcasing new artists. It was large enough to hold a hundred guests but double that number showed up, which told you not only that the opening was a success but also that I had a good chance of finding at least one new client.

Daniel's work interested the press. At first glance the canvases appeared to be collages of photographs of naked female film stars. On closer inspection it became clear that they were actually oil paintings. So the quality of the work, coupled with the number of people drawn to see it, told me that Jennelle would find new clients too.

I took total credit for her outfit: Olive satin D&G pants, a black mesh tank top under a vintage leopard-fur jacket that we had redesigned into a shrug. Whenever someone complimented her, she'd usher that person over to me and say, "Here's my personal shopper and fashion stylist," before she strutted off. I lost count of how many times she did that because the cheap wine made my head feel like it had been dipped into a vat of Ambien. Still, I came away with the names of two women who wanted closet assessments, Jennelle found some potential new artists, and Daniel sold three paintings with expressed interest in several others.

"You didn't meet *anyone*?" Jennelle said, like an overbearing grandmother, when we met in the bathroom as I was standing at the sink, trying to focus my eyes. I shook my head. "Didn't you see that guy with the amazing dark curly hair, in the 'Shit Happens' T-shirt?"

I shook my head.

"Well, what about the hottie with the shirt that said, 'It's Okay, I'll Drop Everything and Help You with *Your* Problem'?"

Another headshake.

"Sage," she said, impatiently. "Weren't you even *trying* to meet someone?"

"The only one I noticed was that tall bimbo with the halter top that made her look naked from the back." She had dark hair that reached her hips, large brown eyes, and heavy eye makeup. "She was hitting on Daniel and everyone else." I couldn't place her cloying perfume, but it reminded me of something that was big in the nineties.

"I saw that, too." Jennelle rolled her eyes. "Her name's Kyla something and she's a big-name rep here and in Europe. She's always in Daniel's store looking for something or other for her artists, but I was talking about guys. Didn't anyone interest you?"

Mostly, I was thinking about Luke Edmond and wondering whether there was any chance he might show up. The art community was small, and word of new shows spread quickly. But by eleven the gallery was almost empty, except for me, Daniel, Jennelle, and Daniel's store manager. We all left together, and then went our separate ways.

Before I mailed my boots to Luke, I called my insurance company and added them to my floater. They cost as much as a piece of jewelry, and I wanted to make sure that if they disappeared, or he did, or if he cut them up and used them in a collage he was making or who knows what else, I wouldn't be left without money to replace them. He was a starving artist without enough money to buy himself dinner. Why should I expect him to send back my precious boots? For all I knew he might now be trying to peddle them on eBay.

I put a note in the box written on fabulous handmade gray paper. I wrote it in red ink from a fountain pen, my way of showing Luke…well, it's obvious, isn't it? Then I waited. The package should have arrived in three days. I hoped that someone wouldn't swipe it if it sat on his front porch.

chapter fifteen

A few weeks after my aborted visit to see Luke Edmond, Mary Alice invited me to spend the weekend with her at the beach. Just thinking about the ocean improved my mood. I packed a few black and white pieces and left by noon. She picked me up from the Hampton Jitney in her *QE II*–sized Chevy Suburban (reverse chic), and we began our meandering— first to a dockside fish store to buy two-pound lobsters and clam chowder, then to the Amagansett farmers' market for salad and fruit as pricey as Fabergé eggs. Our last stop was a bakery in East Hampton for tiny strawberry pastries, still warm, just out of the oven.

"I couldn't live here," I said, brushing crumbs off my pants. "I'd turn into a dough boy."

"You get used to it," Mary Alice said, as we licked our fingers clean before getting back into the car. As we carried the groceries into the kitchen, the dogs—Tarzan and Jane—were at our heels. We uncorked a great Shiraz, lit a fire, and put a pot of water on the stove to boil. Then she gave me the tour.

It reminded me of a visit to a show house. Other than her closet, the master bedroom, and the living room, I hadn't seen the rest of the house. We started by carrying my bag up to one of the guest bedrooms. A dark gray, metal, queen-size Italian canopy bed was in the center, covered with perfectly ironed white linen. The floor was the same French limestone as was throughout the rest of the house. The bed faced the view, and the tall windows on the ocean were framed with puddling white silk drapes tied back with thick pewter cords. There was a mirrored bureau on one wall and on top of it was a heavy crystal vase with white roses. We walked on into the master. It was pale aqua with a full-length Venetian mirror reflecting the ocean. It was festooned with pale turquoise rosettes, probably custom blown to the exact hue of the water. On one side was a sitting area with a turquoise silk couch and two small armchairs.

The third bedroom was icy pink, and a fourth taupe. The bathrooms were all white marble with nickel hardware and double-size Jacuzzi tubs, with windows on the water so that you could look out while you soaked. Each one had perfectly folded white Frette towels with checkerboard borders stacked on the counter next to rectangular bottles of dark green French bath oil.

"Whoever your designer was, I'm in love with her, or him."

"I did a lot of it, but I had different people at different stages," she said. We went back downstairs and I started to walk back toward the fireplace. That's when I noticed the painting that had caught my eye on my first visit. I walked closer to it, feeling the same way I did then. It was abstract, but filled with the colors of the outdoors. It seemed to be lit from within. The first time I saw it I was curious to know who had done it; this time I didn't have to ask.

"Luke Edmond," I said.

She looked up, surprised. "How did you know?"

"You won't believe this," I said, telling her how I found out that he wrote the letter. "But how did you get one of his paintings?"

"He's living on property I bought a few years ago. There's an old farmhouse on it that I was going to tear down so I could build a simple ranch house out there for my mother," she said. "But she died suddenly, a couple of years ago, right after suffering a stroke." She shook her head and her eyes turned moist. "I couldn't face selling the property. I guess it meant letting go, so it sort of languished until one day this fellow called and asked to rent the house. I figured, why not? Only he didn't have much money, so at one point he started doing some gardening for me to make up for not paying the rent."

Bartering, just like Ludwig Bemelmans at the Carlyle.

"When he wanted to go back to painting full-time, he asked if I'd accept a painting in place of six months of rent."

"You got the better deal."

"I didn't realize that at first I just felt sorry for him." She turned to look at the picture again. "But I think you're right. The more that I live with it, the more it grows on me."

I stared at the painting. "I'm surprised he hasn't gotten further with his work."

"He's not what you'd call an aggressive marketer," she said. "From what I can gather, he's kind of quiet and introspective."

I told her about sending him the boots and she laughed. "They'll probably end up in one of his paintings, but you won't know where they are—sort of like *Where's Waldo?*"

"I'm waiting to hear from him—if I do."

"I don't know much about him. He's closer to my dogs. Whenever he comes over they're all over him. They love him."

We went back to the kitchen and tossed the lobsters into the boiling water, then heated the soup, pouring it into tall mugs. "I can't imagine owning a house as fabulous as this one," I said, sipping the creamy chowder as the heat warmed my face. "Please don't take it for granted, Mary Alice. You are blessed."

She gazed out the window and then over at me. "I'm getting better. At first I felt so shaken..." She crossed her arms over her chest. "When you start to accept the idea that you were abandoned and he's not coming back, the resentment sets in. It takes a long time to get over that."

"There's a grieving process. It's like any other major loss."

"You're pretty wise for someone under forty," she said with a laugh. Then her face turned more serious. "It just took me a while to move on from the anger and depression. But now I'm not only accepting it—there are more times than not when I really like being alone. I enjoy my own company." Her eyes twinkled, as if she realized it for the first time.

"I didn't lose a husband of ten years," I said, "but I know what you mean about enjoying your own company. You learn the joys of being single all over again." She bowed her head as if in prayer, and I laughed.

We melted the butter in small white ramekins, made a vinaigrette dressing for the field greens, then took the red potatoes out of the oven. I wasn't one to say grace before every meal, but this time, in this place, it seemed like an affront not to acknowledge what was before us. We savored every morsel of the tender white meat, sending sprays of lobster water across the table at each other.

"Next time I'll put goggles on the table," Mary Alice laughed, pouring out the last drops of wine from the bottle into my glass. "I'll get another," she said, getting up.

There was a piercing wind off the water as we walked along the shore after dinner cocooned in puffy down jackets. We pulled the hoods up and tied them tightly so that the wind didn't steal them from our heads. It felt like we'd landed on an icy moonscape with no one else around. "Any more thoughts on starting your food company?"

"I'm working on some recipes for a horseradish sandwich sauce, and a barbecue sauce with wasabi," she said. "As soon as I've gotten them right, I'm going to look for partners to invest with me and eventually try to find a place out here to set up a kitchen."

"You need a great company name," I said. "The right name and graphics are half of it." Then I glanced back at the house. "But look who I'm telling."

She nodded in agreement. "I've been racking my brain for a good name. I search through magazines, look at food packages, billboards, everywhere." She looked as though she were playing with names in her head. "What do you think of Southampton Kitchen?"

"It conveys the upscale image, but it's not...perfect. And I imagine somebody's already using it for some product or other."

"You're right," she said, as if she were finally crossing

it off the list. "But I know that I'll come up with it. I'm obsessed." We walked on in silence. I stared out at the water in the moonlight, watching the waves. Then it hit me.

"Soupçon."

We both stopped walking. She stared back at me for a long minute, then punched me in the arm. "YES! That's it, that's it." I had never seen Mary Alice's face so animated. I threw my arms around her.

"I'm so proud of you," I said. "You've come so far from the woman I met when I walked into this house." The two of us stared at each other and our eyes welled up with tears. She dropped down in the sand and I sat next to her.

"I realize now that the way you react to a situation is something that is totally up to you," she said, lifting a handful of sand and letting it run through her fingers. "You can fall apart or you can get up and dust yourself off and start having a real life and working toward making yourself happy again. I really do believe that each of us has that ability and it's in our hands."

Somewhere over the past few months, Mary Alice had moved from client to friend—someone I admired and looked up to. Her clearheaded intelligence and can-do spirit boosted mine. I had helped her with clothes and the change helped her get over a rough patch after her breakup, but she had built on that and moved on with her life, beginning it over. Coming up with the company name was like finding her the right dress. It would present the company in the best possible light.

After sipping cordials in front of the fire, we went upstairs to sleep. I looked around the bedroom. How could I have doubted that someone with her vision and intelligence would rebound? The bed was piled with down pillows. There was a fitted sheet over the pillowtop mattress and then a down featherbed with a linen cover over that. Then a top sheet, two down comforters buttoned together, so that if the weather was warm the second one could be removed. The comfort, sensuality, and beauty here were all hers. If that wasn't life affirming... A woman like Mary Alice wouldn't get sidelined for too long. She'd have a better life—she wouldn't stand for less.

I sat in bed under a small pool of yellow light from the bedside lamp, feeling the soft, clean sheet against my bare feet. The sheets were scented with lavender. I turned out the light and the engulfing quiet was like a sleeping potion.

There was a hazy, lemon-yellow light from the morning sun when I woke. I glanced at the small silver clock on the bedside table. Ten. I couldn't remember the last time I'd slept so late. As much as I always missed Harry when he wasn't with me, it was like a vacation to wake up by myself, without his doggy breath in my face at seven when he wanted breakfast. But inexplicably, I turned over, not sure at first why I felt a sinking sensation inside me. I closed my eyes and then I remembered the dream.

I was off in a remote beach house. The only sounds outside were the calls of seagulls and the crashing of waves on the shore. Next to me on the cool white sheets was Luke Edmond.

chapter sixteen

I left on Monday morning. What I really wanted was to stay forever, running on the beach, having lobster dinners, snacking on exquisite pastries, and sleeping on pressed linen sheets while seagulls swirled above my world of water like sentries.

Either Mary Alice was simply the perfect hostess or she was so grateful that I named her company that she got up early enough to have scrambled eggs and smoked salmon waiting. She even packed a lunch for my ride back: a cold steak sandwich dressed with her new horseradish sauce, mango iced tea, and oatmeal cookies. The only thing lacking was a seaplane. I didn't dare joke about it because I knew she'd arrange it.

On my more mundane agenda was finding business suits for a criminal lawyer to soften his image, take-notice outfits for an ebullient writer pitching movie ideas in LA, and more clothes for Brian Schulberg, who, despite the glasses, reported that his date was a huge success.

"Do you believe in love at first sight, Sage?" he asked me, like a sixteen-year-old.

"Hmm, not sure," I said.

"Well I never did, not before. But it happened, I swear. I feel like a goddamned kid."

Success stories like that fueled my ego as I scoured the stores from Missoni, Scoop, and Big Drop to Yves St. Laurent, Armani, Bloomingdale's, Barneys, Bergdorf's, and Saks, and then down to Broadway and Soho boutiques from Vivienne Tam to Yellow Rat Bastard for the quirky find.

"Doesn't it kill you to buy clothes for other people that you can't afford for yourself?" Jennelle said.

"I get a vicarious thrill out of seeing other people wear what I've picked out." It was almost anticlimactic to shop for myself, even though on occasion I splurged on something fabulous like the boots—which reminded me of the dismal fact that almost a month had gone by since I'd sent them to Luke.

Did he get them? Maybe they arrived but he wasn't home and a Long Island felon was strutting around in them playing cowgirl. Or he got them, he painted them, and then he forgot about me. Perhaps he never intended to get in touch with me and return them at all. He might be some weird painter with a foot fetish and he was keeping the boots for his own gratification along with others he had collected from unsuspecting women and now all of them were hidden inside his dank basement. And on and on and on. The possibilities were infinite and I didn't know what to do.

"Just call him," Jennelle said.

"The last time I tried the phone was shut off," I reminded her.

"So go see him again," she said. "Now that you know Mary Alice knows him, tell him you were passing by on your way to see her and wanted to pick them up. They cost a fortune, don't let it slide."

That didn't feel right. The next move was his. I sent him the boots. He promised to return them, and I wanted to wait until he did. But how long? I tried to put things in perspective. They were only boots. Just another possession. Put them out of your mind and focus on things of a higher order. But when you get dressed at least once a day, and then get undressed, it's impossible not to think about what you put on your feet. So I gave him a Friday deadline. If he didn't contact me by then, I'd call. If I had to, I'd visit, but this time I wouldn't bear apples.

Then the mail came. The doorman handed me a box wrapped in brown paper. Unremarkable—until I saw the violet ink along the side of it. I fumbled with my keys and dropped them as I tried to quickly open the three locks. I started to rip open the paper without even giving Harry— now running in circles as if my excitement were contagious— as much as a pat.

I took out the boots and studied them. They looked the same as when I'd sent them. No splattered paint, thank goodness. No smell of linseed oil or anything else an artist used.

And then I saw it.

A white card was wedged into one of the boots. I pulled it out. It was an announcement. In close to three weeks he was having a gallery opening in the Village. On the top of the invitation in violet ink he had printed: "Please come. Wear the boots. L."

Not provocative. Two declarative sentences separated by

a period and a space. So why did I read it again and again as if I hoped to divine some higher meaning? I lifted up the other boot and saw something inside that one too. I pulled out a rolled-up sheet of purple tissue paper. Inside it was a lone sunflower. The colors were perfect together. I took the flower in the paper and tacked it up on my kitchen bulletin board.

Why the sunflower? A thank-you for the loan? Did it mean more? If he couldn't afford a cell, he could have called from a pay phone somewhere. Maybe he preferred nonverbal communication, or he just preferred being an enigma. I needed to call Mary Alice to thank her for the weekend, and now I was glad I had that as an excuse. I wanted to tell her about the boots and see if she was going to his show.

"What show?"

"He's having an exhibit in the Village."

"He didn't tell me. Maybe he just assumed I'd have no interest since I already have a painting and got it by bartering. I suppose he thinks of me as his landlord, not his friend."

I told her about the boots and the sunflower.

"Nice," she said. "Are you interested?"

"I don't know—he's strange."

"Well, he's poor."

"I don't mind that…it's just that he seems to have issues with normal channels of communication."

"He doesn't talk to me a whole lot either," she said, "but when he comes over here now on the rare occasion to work in the garden, he's like the dog whisperer. They seem to relate to him on some higher level. I suppose that means something about his soul."

"It means that maybe I should bark instead of talk. And roll over on my stomach when I see him."

"That might work—it seems to with other men."

The opening was nineteen days away. Because my job was to get people prepared to go anywhere with confidence and style, I should be able to say that *I* didn't spend time worrying about what to wear, especially so far in advance. But it wasn't like that. There are moments when none of us live up to our own hype.

I opened my closet door obsessed with the question of whether tachycardia is considered life-threatening. I took deep breaths. When my heart resumed its normal rhythm, I focused on clothes. The boots, but what else? I wanted to make more of a statement. A white sleeveless undershirt? A white tailored men's shirt? A black tank top? A blazer with nothing under it? I could communicate nonverbally too.

I looked through everything, and then I had it. On a trip to Santa Fe I had found a long-sleeved chamois-colored doeskin shirt that laced up the front. I'd wear it with nothing underneath and leave it unlaced so that I could fill the neck with strands of tiny coral beads, then put a tiny fake rose tattoo slightly to the side of the top of my right breast. Only someone peering into my shirt would see it. Just a detail, but I suspected it would register with Luke Edmond, which reminded me of the sunflower.

I briefly considered sending him a different blossom wrapped inside a sheet of paper with a whimsical note—but I knew I'd end up spending an excruciating amount of time art directing the effort, searching for the right flower and then paper in the perfect hue, not to mention researching whether the flower would survive the trip. Anyway, why mimic him? It was Luke Edmond's turn to wonder if I got the boots and the invitation. If he cared.

chapter seventeen

I had the sense that ever since Jennelle and Daniel fell for each other, they had decided that one of their missions in life was to find someone for me. Was there some imbalance in three people going out together instead of four? Did it violate some intrinsic fêng shui principle of socializing? Not that there was anything wrong with man hunting, it was just that success tended to be serendipitous. Men were like dresses; the perfect ones popped up at unexpected moments, which is why I told my clients *carpe diem*—or seize the perfect dress, in fashion speak, whenever and wherever you saw it.

Not that I kept track of things like the last time I had sex, but in all honesty, I had gone through a pathetically long dry spell—three months plus almost another if you counted the time Greg lived with me and I thought he was suffering from some energy-robbing disease.

I begrudgingly agreed to a blind date with someone Jennelle met in an ad agency. Inevitably, blind dates seemed to have careers that were totally different and incompatible with yours. Say he was a risk analyst, for example, or an investment banker. What would you talk about—your lack of money? Whether you should take out a loan with a fixed rate or an adjustable? Bank robberies? In all probability, he wouldn't have a creative side and the only news he'd focus on would be financial. Otherwise, why would he go into banking? Worse still, what if he wasn't a banker, but an insurance agent? I mean, not counting Wallace Stevens, could it get any bleaker?

So I was soured on blind dates, even though Jennelle assured me that her candidate was not only creative but also hot. He asked her out, but she told him she was seeing someone. Enter Sage Parker.

"What does he look like?"

"Adorable. He wears these round, wire-rimmed glasses, and the day I met him he had on a white suit."

Images of Tom Wolfe passed before my eyes. *A dandy?* I hated that. "Jennelle, I don't think so." I tried to let her down gently. "I'm…I'm just not the white suit type…that's so anal."

"He was dressed up for an advertising awards lunch," she said, waving away my concern.

I was less than excited about the prospect of meeting someone who paraded to work like a Good Humor man, even if it was for a special occasion. "What's his name?"

"Jim. So what about Friday—do you have plans?"

None, except for my annual Pap test. And so the vacillation began. Why not? What do you have to lose? Why yes? What I had to lose that particular Saturday was a free night of HBO. How was I ever going to meet anyone if I was so negative? Why did I prefer to be home alone when I knew if the phone rang at all it would only be Arnie—who I began to think had a crush on me because he called so often. So, suspect as I was, I agreed. Anyway, we were going to a cozy Spanish restaurant in the Village for paella, and I focused on food to nourish my soul.

The good news was that Jim didn't show up in a white suit. The bad news was he arrived in an Irish fisherman's sweater. We weren't meeting on the Dingle Peninsula. What was that about? What's worse, he wore jeans with the wrong belt and the wrong shoes. He needed a thicker belt and heftier shoes or boots. The balance was off, and that was typical of the night.

Perhaps I was obsessed with superficiality, unimportant details that have little to do with character, ethics, and one's overall humanity. But I couldn't help it. I noticed clothes the way a dentist notices teeth. But letting all that slide, although Jim was cute, he had a smile like Homer Simpson, and a laugh that wasn't a laugh.

We all have our signature laughs. They can be deep, throaty, and sensual. Or high-pitched like a drunken eighteen-year-old at a bar. Some laughs make *you* laugh, or invite you to laugh along. Others make you take notice. Or move away.

And Jim's laugh? More of a grunt of irony as though he never let go. That obviously didn't bother the head of his agency where he went from assistant art director to head of creative, responsible for how millions of client dollars were spent for print ads and TV commercials. It was a coup for Jennelle to be socializing with Jim. A nod from him and her clients could be part of megabuck campaigns. And that mattered to me. Still, there were limits to how far a friendship could go.

"Are you going to ask me in?" he said when the cab dropped us in front of my building. Over the past three hours, I'd found out we belonged to different political parties, that he wasn't a dog lover (allergic to them), and not only that we liked different kinds of music (wasn't it time to get over Dave Van Ronk and the Weavers?) but also that he liked swimming in lakes, while I loved the ocean.

"Rain check," I said.

"Pourquoi?"

Pourquoi there's just no chemistry between us and although I'd like to help my friend Jennelle, I can't wait to watch the eleven o'clock news with Harry. "I just had a tough week, but I appreciate the dinner—it was fun."

"Okay," he said, saluting with two fingers before he turned and walked off. The doorman watched with his brows knitted together.

chapter eighteen

The way I looked the night of Luke's gallery opening was no accident. As if the Spartan diet and Herculean exercise regimen weren't enough, I cut out coffee and alcohol for three days because a celebrity circuit aesthetician in LA decreed they were "dehydrating." I got home from work early, fed Harry and walked him. He sensed something was up—probably because I was strutting around the apartment in underwear and the boots instead of barefoot in a bathrobe. A couple of times he jumped up on me the way he does when he wants to let me know he's dying to come along, but I explained that most taxis don't take dogs and anyway, I was not going to a William Wegman show, and this gallery would probably *not* be dog friendly. He dropped to the floor and his downcast eyes followed me around the room.

It was one of those nights when your mind frees you from obsessing about the things you don't like about yourself and you feel good-looking. My hair fell in the way it was supposed to—a millimeter this way or that, it had volume and lift. The color—a shade or two brighter than usual—worked, too. Despite my initial misgivings about whether the highlights looked a tad artificial, or dare I say cheap, I decided they gave subtle variation to my reddish-brown color. With dark brown eyeliner, blusher, and mango Clinique lipstick dotted on to look natural, I was happy with the look. I put on the doeskin shirt (with the rose tattoo, done earlier, peeking out and in just the right spot), the coral beads, Paige jeans, and the boots. Over it, I wore a brown leather jacket with shirred sides that I found at the Porta Portese flea market in Rome.

As I was riding down Second Avenue to White Street in Soho, the cab passed restaurants of every nationality. I wondered how Luke would present himself. Jeans and a denim shirt? Or some costume to make himself stand out? The purple ink and the blue stationery made me think he would come up with something.

The driver stopped on a dark street lined with industrial buildings. Behind the old warehouse facades were chic multimillion-dollar lofts that most artists could no longer afford. The street was deserted except for a cyclist with a messenger bag slung across his chest. I looked up and saw a white banner about seven feet long hanging off a balcony. In script, large turquoise letters read: LUKE EDMOND: SELECTED PAINTINGS.

I paid the driver, walked up a few steps to the entrance, and pulled open a heavy black iron door. I walked past mailboxes with names hand-printed on yellow paper and a small freight elevator. I decided to walk the four long flights of steep steps. I opened the heavy black iron door that led to a gallery with bright lighting and twenty-foot ceilings. The walls were a ghostly white and the ceiling was black with a glass skylight covered with chicken wire. The gallery was packed with a Felliniesque assortment of downtown types as though central casting had assembled the standard-issue group of gallery visitors: Guys in their thirties with long hair in black jeans and turtlenecks; women in long, baggy skirts wearing oversized artsy earrings and necklaces that I guessed they had either made themselves or bought from someone they knew. There was a girl about my age who had short, spiky, hot pink hair who stood with a group of pale, sensitive, macrobiotic types who looked like they needed blood. I went to the far end of the room, found a clear plastic cup, and poured myself white wine. Then I scanned the gallery.

I spotted Luke from the back. He was wearing a beige cotton sport jacket drip painted yellow and green à la Jackson Pollock. When he turned to the side, I saw a grass-green T-shirt underneath it. Jeans, torn at one knee.

Perfect.

His hair hung straight, parted on the side. I stared at his profile. Straight nose, prominent jawline, the shadow of a beard. He was talking with someone in a well-cut navy suit with a lavender tie—probably a collector. I watched them, and then went to look at the paintings.

The gallery was made up of two adjacent rooms and Luke's canvases were spread out—three on each wall. The impact of seeing them all perfectly lit was almost visceral. They were all very different, but done with the same bold brushstrokes and vibrant mixes of color, like a glorious marriage of Joan Mitchell and Franz Kline. Purple and red, or green and yellow. Another blue and purple with touches of green. Every painting seemed to have scintillating accent colors—fuchsia, daffodil, coral, as if to show the viewer the small wonders that nature held in store. He saw deep into his surroundings, and he wanted his paintings to show not only what the natural world looked like but also the forces behind it. It looked as if Luke were intoxicated with the beauty when he lifted his brush.

I wanted to tell him how thrilled I was by his work, but someone else got there before me. She was as tall as he was in her black high-heeled slingbacks. The filmy, low-cut black dress showcased her cleavage, framed by an orange shawl around her shoulders that matched three heavy coral and gold bangle bracelets on her arm.

I had seen her before, but I couldn't place her. She leaned close to him and whispered in his ear before strutting off. Then she seemed to think better of it and went back, leading him by the hand over to a well-dressed couple. Did she work for one of the designers I knew? Did I know her face from TV? I remembered once seeing someone in a restaurant who looked so familiar that I went up to her and asked her where I knew her from. She was an anchor on the news, she said. I laughed, embarrassed, and walked off.

But something about this woman's authoritative air was familiar to me. Then it struck me. Daniel's opening. Jennelle said she was an artist's rep. I looked at her from a distance. She reached over to Luke and put her arm around his shoulders proprietarily as though he was the star and she was working the room with him. Would I even get a chance to say more than hello?

As it got more crowded, it got warmer and closer inside. I took off my jacket and continued my stroll around, looking at the paintings while almost involuntarily glancing behind me to find Luke. There was a split second when he was alone and I turned toward him. He looked up and saw me, his mouth curving up into a small smile. I watched him glance down momentarily, noticing my boots, and then we started toward each other simultaneously.

"Thanks for coming," he said, his eyes holding mine. He ran a finger up the sleeve of my shirt to feel my skin.

"The paintings are extraordinary. I love your work."

He looked slightly flustered. "Thanks. Well...let's hope some of them sell."

I wanted to buy all of them, but afraid of sounding like a gushing fan, I didn't say that. "Is this your first show?"

He nodded. "Someone's repping me, finally." He gestured as though the show were beyond him. "She set this up." An older woman with a tight gray bun walked up to him and peered through steel-framed glasses as though he were something on display. "Luke?" He turned and nodded. "I'm with *Art News*, Kyla told me about you." Kyla. Now I remembered. Jennelle had mentioned her name.

"I'd love to get some more information on your background," she said. "I'm doing a roundup of new artists." I turned to leave so he could talk without me hovering.

"You're not going yet, are you?" He reached out and touched my shoulder.

"No...I'll stay for a while."

"Please...I need to talk to you." He glanced back at the woman momentarily. "Just as soon as we're through."

As I walked around, I tried not to keep turning to keep track of him. I went back to the wine table for a refill, scooping up some pretzels. Just as I was turning away from the table, I felt a hand on my shoulder and I almost jumped.

"Sage?"

I turned and came face-to-face with Jordan.

"Hello again," I said. This time she was wearing the Burberry quilted jacket in cornflower blue. "How are you?"

She nodded. "So you found your mystery man."

"Yes, thanks to you. Actually, it turned out that the house he's living in is owned by a client of mine."

"Six degrees," she said. I turned to look at the girl she was with. She was thin, almost boyish, with short, wispy hair, fine features, and deep blue eyes.

"This is Caroline," Jordan introduced us. "And this is Sage Parker. She knows Thomas."

I smiled and looked at Jordan uncertainly. I was sure that she had told me that Caroline had gotten married. She looked back at me and laughed. "Another Caroline. So, what do you think of his paintings?" she said, changing the subject.

"They're astonishing—he's so talented."

She shook her head in agreement. "I always thought so, but I guess he needed someone with a business head to set things in motion for him," she said, gesturing toward the dark-eyed woman.

I thought of Jennelle. Maybe she should spend time with this über-agent.

"Really," I said, too earnestly.

She looked down at my boots. "I was out at his place and saw him painting those. I didn't realize that they were yours."

"I went out to see him. He was pretty taken with the boots."

She looked at me for a long minute, narrowing her eyes.

"Do you like him?"

I stared back, uncomfortable with the question. "I don't know him."

She leaned over and kissed my cheek. "You will," she said, taking Caroline by the arm as they walked off.

I didn't want to interrupt him while he was being interviewed. This was his chance to get publicity, but it seemed as though she were spending enough time with him to write his life story. Kyla didn't keep her distance, though. She waltzed up to them smiling broadly, putting her arm around Luke's waist and pulling him toward her.

Was he sleeping with her? Or was she just like that? Maybe it was her way with the people whose lives she was in charge of. I couldn't pick up any body language from Luke that showed he felt close to her. He didn't sling an arm around her waist or give her an affectionate kiss. Perhaps Jordan knew. She seemed to be intimately familiar with his life.

Rather than wandering aimlessly, I made an effort to talk to people. I complimented someone in a black satin baseball jacket on his pop art tie with a pinball machine on it. He reminded me of a rock star promoter. We got into a discussion of downtown rents.

"I got a place down on Greene Street a few years ago," he said. "Two thousand square feet, but a wreck. I paid close to a million then. Now it's worth over six." Clearly it was no neighborhood for starving artists.

"How do you know Luke?" I asked, changing the subject to something with more possibility.

"I don't. I'm Kyla's friend. I go to all of her shindigs."

"She must have quite a stable of artists."

"She knows everybody," he said. "If she's into what you do, she opens doors for you."

I glanced over his shoulder and saw Luke looking at me. I smiled and he headed over to me, taking my arm. "Excuse me," I said, walking off. Luke led me to a side door. "Where are we going?" I asked, following him out.

"I wanted to talk to you for a minute without getting pulled away," he said. "Do you mind?" I shook my head. We stood outside the studio on the top of a black metal fire escape that led to a small alleyway. It was dark except for a streetlight that cast a yellow pool of light down on the sidewalk. I thought of Edward Hopper.

"I want to paint the boots again," he said, softly.

"Now?" I joked.

He shook his head. "I want to paint them—on you."

"Oh." Suddenly I was flustered. "I don't know. I've never…modeled or anything."

"All you have to do is sit there. It's not a figure-drawing thing. You don't have to take off your clothes. I just want to paint you wearing them."

From the first time I spoke to Luke Edmond I noticed that when he talked to you he looked hard into your eyes as though he were searching for information—or looking into your head. Was it only with me or did he do that with everyone? Was he just stone-cold sober serious? His face was close to mine and it occurred to me that he might try to kiss me. I waited, struck by his odd mix of directness and elusiveness. I looked away first. He obviously wasn't thinking about kissing me; he was waiting for an answer. "When?"

"In a couple of weeks. I'm going to Paris tomorrow, so when I get back."

"Nice. R&R?"

"No, I'm having a show there. I can't believe any of this, but it's in an important gallery, I'm told. I'm supposed to be excited about it."

"But you're not." I said it more as a statement than a question.

He scratched the side of his neck. "I don't know... it's weird."

"How?"

He shrugged. "I'm used to being anonymous, so..."

"Your paintings are wonderful. You deserve the attention."

"Well, I need the money. I'm so broke..." He didn't finish the sentence.

I leaned over and kissed his cheek and he took his fingertips and ran them up and down the side of my face, then stared down at me briefly.

"I like the rose," he said, almost guiltily.

"I like your jacket." Neither of us spoke for a long moment.

He ran a hand through his hair. "I better get back." His voice was low, almost hoarse. "They'll think I ran out." He held the door open and followed me in. I squinted in the bright light. I turned slightly and saw someone standing a few steps from the door. When my eyes adjusted, I saw the orange shawl.

chapter nineteen

It was a Friday night and my plan was to get into a bath with a glass of wine and a book. All I was concerned with was unwinding. I was tempted not to answer the phone when it rang. They'd call back if it was important. But after two rings, I leapt toward it.

"Hey."

My heart quickened before my head realized who it was. I felt as though I were caught reading his diary. "Hey back."

A soft laugh. "It's Luke."

"Oh." I put some surprise in my voice. "How was Paris?"

"My head's still spinning, but maybe that's from not sleeping." There was a pause. "I sold some paintings...and got some good press...I guess it was worth it."

"I'm glad," I said, not sure what he was really saying. "I'm happy you called." The words spilled out before I could weigh them. Then there was a tiny awkward blip of silence that I was beginning to think was typical of the way Luke communicated.

"Do you think that you could come out here?" he blurted out.

"Well, when?"

"Tomorrow?"

Did he think I was just sitting around waiting for him to call? I thought of saying that next week was better. "I guess I could drive out," my voice answered.

"That would be great."

He was ready to hang up. "Wait," I said, too frantically. "What time is good?"

"Anytime."

"All right, but I have to bring Harry."

"Who?"

He didn't know about Harry, I realized then. "He's my dog. I can't leave him home alone all day."

"Oh, sure." He sounded relieved. "Bring Harry, I'd love to meet him."

"Okay then." I placed the receiver back carefully and refilled my glass, holding it up to toast an invisible partner.

• • •

Fortunately, Harry was a great traveler. He climbed into the back seat and fell asleep. I remembered reading an article about traveling with pets that said the wonderful thing about them is they never ask, "Are we there yet?" When they're with you, they're there.

We drove out on a cold December morning under a gray sky. I was in jeans, the boots, and a black turtleneck sweater under a black down North Face jacket. Knowing how bare Luke's cupboard had been the last time I was there, I was tempted to pack tea bags, cookies, or at least cheese and fruit, but no, I wasn't his mother. It wasn't my place to feed him or stock his refrigerator. Now that he had sold some of his paintings, he could afford lunch.

I pulled up to his house and stopped the car. "This is it, Harry. I hope you like him." I got out and let Harry out of the back door. Luke stepped out on the porch right then, as if he'd been listening for us, and Harry bolted over to sniff him. Luke kneeled and Harry nearly toppled him, licking his face. Luke murmured to him and scratched Harry's head, which was a signal for him to get down and roll onto his back so Luke could scratch his stomach.

"He's easy." Luke smiled up at me and I tried to pretend I wasn't struck by how good he looked in a black T-shirt and jeans that outlined his lean thighs. He got to his feet and came over, giving me a brief hug. Then he studied me. "Come in the house," he said, finally.

Mary Alice was right to think of tearing it down and starting over for her mother. It looked as if it belonged to someone's dead grandmother. There was a sagging blue couch, an overstuffed club chair, a utilitarian brown wooden coffee table, and a braided rug over a linoleum floor. It was depressing, really. There was a wooden table and two blue chairs in the middle of the small kitchen. Mary Alice obviously hadn't sent her decorator here. Did Luke see how sad the house was?

He opened a cabinet and took out two glasses. "Juice?" I nodded and he poured two glasses of apple juice. He carried them to the couch and we sat down. "I want to paint you outdoors," he said, without any preliminaries. "I know it's cold, but…"

"It's okay, I'll let you know when my heart stops and my blood freezes." I looked down at my jeans. "Is this outfit okay?"

"Wait," he said. He left the room and came back with a bag. Inside it was a coral-colored skirt with a ruffle around the hem. He held it out to me. "I bought this in Paris. I thought of you and the boots when I saw it."

"Pretty. Maybe you can join me in my business."

"What do you do?"

"I'm a wardrobe consultant."

He nodded. "That fits," he said, ending the discussion. He went over to a closet and took out a jean jacket. "Maybe this over it?" I slipped it on. It was obviously his, so it was too big for me. I rolled up the sleeves.

"Take off the sweater. Let the tattoo show."

Now I would really freeze. "The tattoo is gone."

He looked concerned for a moment and shook his head, not understanding.

"It wasn't real," I almost laughed. "It was one of those ink transfer tattoos that you press on."

His face fell like a little boy who's told there's no more ice cream. "Oh," he said. He stared off, lost in thought for a moment. "Wait," he said, holding up a hand. He went out of the house, walking toward his studio. A few minutes later he was back with three tubes of paint, a wooden palette, and two brushes.

"Take off your sweater," he said, casually.

I cocked my head to the side. "What for?"

"I'm putting the rose back."

I looked at him, unsure. I wasn't ready to get undressed in front of him. I went into the bathroom and came back wearing the skirt with the jacket over my bra. I pulled half of the jacket open.

"Pull aside the bra," he said, putting the wooden handle of the brush between his teeth as he opened a tube of paint.

I was blushing like a twelve-year-old, so he'd been successful in turning me into a modest little mouse. "Forgive me...but I'm just not used to having strange men paint roses on my breasts."

"Sorry," he said, taking the brush out of his mouth. He smiled, breaking the tension. "I didn't mean to make you uncomfortable. I just thought it was perfect on you when I saw it at the show. We can skip it, if you'd rather."

I slipped the strap off my shoulder so that half of my right breast was exposed. "Go ahead, but I have to warn you that I might laugh if the brush tickles."

There was a serious expression on his face as he mixed the paints. "I'll try to make it fast." Clearly there was nothing sexual about it to him. It was just another thing to paint. I stared down at the floor while he used just the tip of a fine brush and made a few short strokes. I was aware of the strong scent of the oil paint. I wondered if he still noticed it.

"There. But you won't be able to touch it for a while. Oil paint doesn't dry quickly."

I'd be sitting out in the freezing cold, half naked, while Luke painted me. "This is really lunacy. I don't even know what I'm doing here."

"You're here because you're beautiful and I'm painting you." He looked slightly annoyed that there was anything to discuss. "And the boots are who you are so I wanted to paint you wearing them."

How did I answer that? I shrugged. "So let's get started."

He put two chairs together outside. I sat back in one

and propped my feet up on the other, pulling my skirt back so that the boots showed. He sat opposite me on a stool and quickly sketched with a pencil in a large white pad. I had no sense of how much time had passed. I was afraid to steal a look at my watch. But at some point, half an hour, or possibly more, I was aware I'd lost sensation in my fingers. One of them had turned white and I couldn't bend it. How was he able to keep sketching?

"Luke, I'm frozen…we have to stop."

He didn't answer. Did he hear me? "Luke," I said again.

"Just another minute," he said, without focusing on me. I waited. One minute, two, but he didn't stop. Finally I got up and went into the house, slipping into my jacket while trying to keep it away from the rose. I'd been flattered that he wanted to paint me at first. Now I was just annoyed. He came in a few minutes later.

"I'm sorry, I get lost sometimes when I work. It's selfish." He shook his head. I didn't answer and he went over to the fireplace and threw on a few logs and some twigs. He kneeled and struck a match and tossed it in. There was a crackling sound as the wood caught fire, giving the room a warm glow.

"Sit here," he said, pulling a blanket off the couch and spreading it in front of the fire. "You'll be warm in a minute." He sat down and smiled at me.

"Tea would help. Do you have any?"

He went into the kitchen and came back and holding up a tin. Fauchon Matin de France. "This okay?"

"Yes, fine." I heard him turn on the water and I stared into the fire. Just weeks before he had been penniless, now he was buying Fauchon? A gift for someone? He came back in and handed me a large white ceramic mug.

I closed my hands around it to warm them and took a sip. "It's delicious."

We sat staring into the hypnotic flames without talking. The house was freezing. How could he stand it? I moved closer to the fire and looked at Luke. Sometimes I felt I knew him intimately, other times he was a total stranger. He could be warm or cold. He sat there without speaking and then reached for a poker and stirred the logs. One fell with a soft thud and a tiny explosion of sparks flew like pixie dust.

"Are you always so chatty?"

He stared at me shyly and smiled briefly. I looked away. "Tell me more about Paris." How fortunate I wasn't a talk show host who had to interview him. He gave me a sideward glance and raised an eyebrow.

"If I could read the reviews I guess I'd know more about what they thought of me." He shrugged. "But I was told they liked the paintings. I even sold some."

"So now you can eat."

"It's nice to be able to pay the rent and buy food—and paint. I've used up my credit everywhere."

"I'm glad for you; you deserve it. You have such a gift." He sat back with his arms crossed over his knees and his chin pressed against the top of his arm.

"When you're starving for so long, you start to doubt anybody will ever see anything in what you do. Then you think there's a reason nobody sees anything. Why paint when you're not able to reach people? You become an outcast, you question your vision, your talent, you question your whole existence, but still you do it and you can't imagine life if you couldn't." He looked at me almost imploringly. "Does any of that make any sense to you?"

"I imagine every creative person goes through that. It's your rite of passage. You're just one of a long line of starving artists who's finally getting noticed." I stretched my legs out so my feet were closer to the fire. "You're in good company." I shrugged. "Maybe it's good to struggle first—it humbles you. It's not meant to be easy. It would be a travesty if it was."

He nodded, staring into my eyes, almost childlike, completely unselfconscious. I looked down when he didn't.

"Warming up?" He reached over and pulled my jacket closer around me.

"Yes." I looked at him warily when I saw him glance outside. "Don't tell me we have to go out again?"

He bit his bottom lip. "We have to go out again."

"I'm a terrible model, I'm sorry; I get so grouchy when I'm cold. Maybe if you were Gauguin and we were in the tropics, I'd be more amenable."

"Then you'd complain about the heat."

"I'm not going," I pretended to hide my head under my arms.

"C'mon," he said, "just don't think about the cold." He rose to his feet and reached for my hand to pull me up. "It's mind over matter, and anyway, the light's so good now."

"You're a sadist."

He gave me a half smile. "It turns women on." I was about to object, but he was already out the door.

I climbed back into the cold metal chair, stretching my legs out. This time I didn't take off my jacket and Luke didn't say anything. "How often do you use models?"

Did he hear me? I repeated the question.

"Not often," was the clipped response.

"Do you use live plants?" My idea of a joke. Again, no answer. I considered sticking my tongue out at him to see if that brought a reaction. I had assumed we would talk while he worked and get to know each other, but just the opposite seemed to happen. I was transformed from a person into a physical object. He seemed to lose himself, looking at me so hard I was sure he wasn't seeing me at all because he was fixated on what was in his head. Talk distracted him, so I didn't make any other efforts. Finally I saw him glance up at the sky and then back at me. He got down from the stool, shaking his head as though he were annoyed. Was it me?

"We're done." He nodded as though a business meeting were over. He strode back into the house, leaving me sitting there.

"Am I dismissed?"

"What?" He looked bewildered. Obviously he had no idea what I was annoyed about and he wasn't even focusing on it. His eyes held mine.

"I wasn't getting what I wanted," he said, exasperated, as if he were talking to himself as much as to me. "And now the light is gone, the moment is over, and it won't be the same ever again and you've lost something you saw because you couldn't get it down." He searched my face to see if I understood. *No, I don't understand your frustration,* I wanted to say, but I tried to have an expression that was neutral, as though I were taking in what he said and considering it rather than dwelling on how selfish and shallow I was because all I was thinking about was sitting out in the cold, freezing, and that had nothing to do with his picture.

Not knowing what else to do or say, I went into the bathroom and changed back into my sweater and jeans. I folded the skirt and left it on the side of the sink. When I went back into the living room he was in front of the fire. Harry was stretched out next to him, as if Luke were his best buddy. It annoyed me. How dare he cozy up to Luke? He had just met him. So much for dogs being loyal.

I glanced at my watch: almost four. "I'll be heading back." I couldn't tell whether the tension, big as an elephant, was totally in my head, or whether his frustrations with his work had come between us.

Luke looked up. "We'll start again tomorrow." He scratched the side of his head as if he were coming to terms with the fact that he had to start over.

"What?"

"What time can you come back?"

Anger was rising up my spine. It felt like he was talking to a plumber who had to return to finish a job. "Tomorrow?"

"In the morning?" If he picked up on my annoyance, he ignored it.

"It's a long drive," I said, dismissively. Another uncomfortable pause. I just wanted to get out the door and leave.

"You can stay if you want," he said, tentatively.

There was nothing in his tone that told me he wanted me to stay or cared in the least. It was just a cold, last-minute accommodation, and that made it worse than if he didn't ask. "I have to feed Harry and do things at home." I paused. "And I'm meeting a friend for dinner." Why did I come up with that?

"The weather will be warmer tomorrow," he tried.

"If I can." I put on Harry's leash and tugged him toward the door.

Harry was asleep as soon as I started the car. As I pulled out, I glanced back at the house through the rearview mirror. Luke was watching me from the open doorway.

chapter twenty

I'm not sure how the conversation started, but a shrink I was seeing after a painful breakup with a boyfriend told me I obsessed about small, unimportant details. She said it in an almost accusatory way, as though it were part of a personality disorder. I didn't agree then, but driving home with the sun getting lower and the sky growing smoky dark, it occurred to me that she might be right, because I was fixating on the black tin of Fauchon tea with the yellow logo. It was just a stupid, unimportant, overpriced tin of tea, something he could have gotten anywhere—still, it didn't strike me as something Luke would buy. Fauchon tea went with Frank Cooper's marmalade, the queen's favorite, and French roast coffee. It went with smoked salmon and kippered herring. It wasn't a staple in the kitchen of a man who went to bed without dinner because he couldn't afford food. I noticed it the way I would have if I had been watching a movie about a poor family and saw a Baccarat vase in the living room.

It occurred to me then that he didn't even make a cup

for himself. He was probably a coffee drinker. If that were the case, how did it get there and who was it for? He had just come from Paris and it was a new tin, so more than likely it was bought there. So now Kyla was in the picture. Assuming she bought it, how did it end up in Luke's house? Was she out there? Did she drop it off? Did she have it in the morning for breakfast? The more I thought about that scenario, the more likely it appeared. They probably went shopping together in Paris, she bought the tea and left it at his house so she could have it for breakfast. She had probably been to his house before. She knew the kitchen cabinets would be empty. No wonder Luke showed no interest in me, other than the perfunctory compliment to keep me posing for him—he was sleeping with her.

I should have snooped around—checked the medicine cabinet or the bathroom closet. Maybe I would have seen a robe. I imagined her wrapping herself in a flowing black silk kimono she bought on a trip to Japan, or a long white robe of Italian silk from Como. More likely she didn't have anything other than the clothes she wore when she got there. They made love, she stayed over and wore his shirt. There was probably one hanging somewhere with her perfume on it. The name of her fragrance came to me then—Guerlain's Nahema—heavy, floral, with hyacinth and rose. More complex and Old World than the beachy or citrus scents women like me wore. Someone I knew who worked at Bergdorf's used it. It was provocative, like Kyla.

I fed Harry when I got home, then climbed into a hot bath and stayed under water until my fingers shriveled. Going out there and seeing him was worse than not going. I turned off the light by nine. I hadn't done anything more strenuous than sitting and then driving home. Why did I feel so exhausted and beaten down?

In the morning I sat up in bed and stared out the window at the high-rise across the street. Cars battling their way up Third Avenue announced themselves with blasts from their horns. A fire engine made sure no one slept late.

I thought about Luke in his house on Long Island. How would it be to wake up out there—in his bedroom? Where would I have slept? Would anything have happened?

• • •

Between the hours of nine and ten, when most people were asleep, out running, or just lounging at home and reading the paper, I was playing mind games with myself.

The hell with him, I wouldn't go back there.

I would. I agreed to let him paint me. He needed to finish.

He kept me out in the cold, oblivious to everything except his sketchbook. I was an object. Go all the way back like someone with no self-respect?

Was he really so bad? Maybe that was my slanted take on it. Or maybe he really was cold and indifferent. Or he didn't like the way his sketches were going. Or he didn't like his model. It didn't matter. I looked at the clock and thought about going back to sleep versus lining up at Avis and punching myself up for another long afternoon of sitting out in the cold. I pulled up the blanket and the decision made itself.

chapter twenty-one

Weeks went by and Arnie and I had dinner together a few times. I surprised myself by being close-mouthed about the whole Luke saga. Instead of eating in, we decided we needed a "feed," so we went to the famed 2nd Avenue Deli, not on 2nd Avenue and Tenth Street in the East Village anymore, but now on East 33rd, between Lexington and Third.

No New York deli fan can forget the story of the beloved owner, Abe Lebewol, who opened it in 1954 and was known for his generosity in feeding the needy. When he was murdered in 1996 on his way to make a deposit in the bank, it shocked New Yorkers and made headlines. The case was never solved.

Arnie and I gorged ourselves on oversized pastrami and corned beef sandwiches, potato knishes, great coleslaw, and sour pickles. Just as the check arrived, Arnie turned to me. There was an expression on his face I'd never seen before.

"I think I met someone."

I looked up, surprised. "Way to go, buddy," I said, a bit

too enthusiastically. "Who is she?"

"She works in my office."

I had been sure he'd say he met her online and I'd been about to give him an I-told-you-so. "A new hire?"

He shook his head. "She's worked there for almost as long as I have, and I don't know whether she got a new haircut or something, but we were in the cafeteria line together and we started to talk about the way they didn't change the oil enough when they fried the flounder."

I lifted my eyebrows, but I didn't want to stop him.

"We ended up having lunch together and I asked her if she wanted to have dinner someplace where the fried fish was fresh. I've seen her a few times since."

"Great, Arnie, I hope it works out for you." Then the little bee stings of jealousy. Now even Arnie had met someone. Jennelle had Daniel. Even Mary Alice was no longer home alone watching the seagulls. She was in the city meeting a male friend who was taking her to dinner and to the Public Theater. Just a friend, but nonetheless an evening out with a member of the opposite sex. And the great makeover queen? Miss Look Perfect Anytime, Anywhere? Home with a DVD from Netflix. At this rate, the Academy of Motion Picture Arts and Sciences would anoint me master of filmography.

"So you didn't even need new clothes," I said, making myself feel even worse. "She likes you for who you are."

"Well, I did buy the suit you sent me the picture of," he said, brightening my spirits somewhat. "And I tried to buy the tie too, but they were sold out."

"You should have told me. I could have gotten it for you wholesale. What's her name?" I asked for no particular reason.

"Brie."

I had trouble with certain names, particularly if they were usually attached to things like cheese, rather than people. (Yes, sage is a cooking herb, but it's more common.) Or, for that matter, if the names were not gender specific (Jordan, for example), leading to the obvious questions.

"Maybe her mother had a craving for brie during her pregnancy?" I couldn't resist.

"Actually, yes—no, I have no idea," Arnie said, smoothing his hair. I was making him uncomfortable.

"I'm happy for you. I'd love to meet her."

"I'm making her dinner one night next week. I'll let you know when so you can come up."

• • •

Jennelle emailed me a picture of Luke. It was part of a short item about his show that ran on a downtown paper's website. I considered printing it out and remembered a friend of mine told me about a psychic who could tell you about your life without meeting you—even if you lived far away—if she had a recent picture of you.

Unsettling was the word that came to mind when I thought of Luke. There was this tension. But was it because he was ill at ease with everybody, or just with me? I stared at the picture. The streaked blond hair, the barest smile. Shyness? Arrogance? Insolence? He never called after I left his house. Would he write? Was he waiting for me to call him?

The first thing he should have done was ask me to have dinner, showing warmth, caring, personal interest to make me feel like a person, not an object in a still life, a pear in a bowl of fruit. So one day if it wasn't there, it could be replaced by an apple. A fig. No big deal.

Days passed and I went from client to client, closet to closet, putting other people's lives back on track, ordering their chaos, listening to their frustrations, and helping them become who they could be. Sometimes the benefits of helping others were enough. But not now. My work was hard. It wasn't glamorous, despite what people thought.

Shopping all day? So fun!

Some days, in fact, I felt like a servant: hooking people's bras, pulling up their panties, and helping them on with their shoes like a supplicant.

It came as no surprise one morning that I felt a scratchy feeling in the back of my throat. I rummaged through my bag and realized I didn't have any zinc lozenges. To make matters worse, I was in Soho after meeting a model who needed clothes for her honeymoon. She was always dressed by magazine stylists and designers, she said, but when she had to dress herself, especially for an important occasion, she was completely at a loss.

I was walking down Broadway a few days after we had snow. Much of it was piled on the sides of the street, but there was still a thin layer of ice coating the sidewalk. I took small, baby steps, as if I were playing Simple Simon, taking care not to slip. Very few people were outside. Lower Manhattan seemed to have its own rhythm, not getting up and joining the world until almost lunchtime. Just as I approached the subway, I looked up when I heard the sound of a heavy metal door on an industrial building slamming closed. A woman with long, dark hair walked out. She was wearing a full-length sable coat. She had a long orange scarf wrapped several times around her neck. In her hand was a burnt orange Kelly bag. A moment later, someone tall and blond in a brown leather bomber jacket followed her out. Just before I went down the staircase, I looked back once more and realized who it was.

Luke.

chapter twenty-two

Jennelle's fifties-style red Formica kitchen was now her office. She couldn't afford a real space yet, but that didn't matter because she wasn't at the stage where she needed a place to bring clients. She had only two—actually, three—clients, if you counted Daniel. One was a graphic designer, and the other an illustrator. She spent hours each day visiting art directors at publishing houses for the illustrator and then advertising agencies for the graphic designer, talking up her people and trying to network with the art community. Plus, she spent time trying to woo new artists whose work both she and Daniel thought was fresh and exciting.

After a month, she got the designer a job on a Lysol campaign with a leading agency. The illustrator hadn't gotten anything yet, but samples of his work were in the hands of art directors whose job it was to pick illustrators for book covers. It was slow going and she was living off her savings.

"I'm giving it a year or two," she said. "After that, I'll have to look for other work if my income doesn't grow." She told me about some gallery openings she had been to, since she was now making the rounds to meet new artists, but it was like the catch-22 field of acting. You couldn't get jobs unless you had experience, but how did you get experience if you had no track record and no one was willing to give you work? Still, some new artists figured they had nothing to lose by signing on with someone who had more energy than experience. In the meantime, she was taking out small ads on targeted websites, and starting her own website. I became a client and we found a couple of other friends in art or related fields who said they'd lend their names to make her client list look more impressive. She even put an item on Craigslist. Of course, that seemed to bring out a lot of self-styled artists who had more nerve than talent.

Jennelle, Daniel, and I were sharing a pizza in the Village before heading to the Angelika for a movie. "Guess who I saw the other morning?" I said.

"I give up," Jennelle said.

"The über-agent." I didn't say that Luke was with her.

Jennelle scrunched up her nose. "Kyla's not exactly someone I'd like to model myself after."

I took another bite. "What do you mean?"

"She knows how to use her feminine wiles," she said, taking a slice of pepperoni off her pizza and putting it onto Daniel's.

I turned to Daniel. "I saw her coming on to you."

"I didn't notice her cleavage, I swear," he said, straight-faced.

"I imagine Luke did." I smiled tightly. "They must have had a cozy time in Paris."

"Luke Edmond?"

I nodded.

"He was in the store last week," he said. "I realized I had met him before. He put up some kind of notice on the bulletin board."

"What did it say?" I asked, almost to myself.

"Dunno. I didn't look. Is he looking to move or rent his place?"

"Not as far as I know, but maybe I should call him and pretend I saw his note. Get him to drive in from Long Island on some pretext, and then drive all the way back. Maybe he enjoys driving five hours in one day."

"What did he do to you?" Daniel said, narrowing his eyes.

"He messed with her head," Jennelle said, in an exaggerated Southern accent.

"He has a boot fetish," I explained, "but it ends at the knees, I think, because that's where he cut me off."

Daniel pressed his fingers against his eyelids. "We can't win. If we jump your bones you don't like it, but if we don't come on to you, you don't like it either."

"So you're taking his side—thank you, Daniel, thanks for the support." Daniel took out his wallet to pay for the pizza.

"Thanks for the slice, anyway."

He put his arm around me and hugged me. "Don't worry, Sagey. The man will come to his senses. You're a hottie."

"He's sleeping with Kyla. He's not thinking about me."

"But she's also sleeping with Edward what's-his-name, the one whose pictures look like Rothkos," Jennelle said.

"Scissorhands?" Daniel asked.

"How do you know *that*?" I asked. "Art world internet chatter?"

"I had lunch with Edward," Jennelle said. "She doesn't wear underwear."

I squeezed my eyes shut. "Spare me."

"No shit," Daniel said. "Why didn't you tell *me* that?"

"Daniel," Jennelle said, "please shut up."

• • •

We headed to the Angelika to buy tickets for *Belle de Jour* and lined up outside. It was eight and the movie was starting at eight fifteen. I pulled up the collar of my jacket and tied my scarf around my neck. When I looked up, I was face-to-face with Greg. It took a moment to register.

"Sage," he said. He was as surprised as I was.

"How's it going?" I asked, buying time.

"Good—I'm working on a new flick about women in prison. I'm really excited about it. Thanks for asking."

"I'm glad for you. How's Pompidou?" I asked, nearly choking on the ludicrous name of my replacement.

He shrugged. "Ah, that's...that's over," he said, momentarily looking down. He opened his mouth to say something else, but then he obviously thought better of it. "What about you?"

"I'm good." I bobbed my head as if it were spring-loaded. "Busy."

"You seeing anyone?"

I hesitated, knowing that I had seconds to decide whether I wanted to leave the door open or close it in his face. I took a step closer and looked up at him. "Actually, yes." I smiled to tell him that was all I wanted to say.

"Good," he said, patting my arm stupidly. "I'm happy

for you." He walked to the end of the line and Jennelle and I exchanged glances. She pretended to inhale from a cigarette and then exhaled dramatically. "Au revoir, Pompidou," she whispered in an exaggerated French accent.

chapter twenty-three

The day before Christmas, a client gave me a large shopping bag with two presents inside. Both were wrapped in leopard-print paper. I opened them up and found a sweater for me and a dog collar and leash for Harry. But just not a dog collar and a leash—a collar and leash in the signature tan plaid of Burberry.

The problem was that Harry's neck was bigger than the collar—equivalent to a man with a 16-inch neck getting a shirt with a 14½-inch collar. So I went back to the store to exchange it, only to find they were out of the larger collars. Then I remembered who worked for Burberry. Call or not call? I played with the idea for a nauseating amount of time. Finally I stopped. *Fuck it*, I said to myself.

"Hey, Sage," Jordan said, when I phoned. "Do you want to have lunch?" We met in a Greek restaurant near Carnegie Hall. I was confused for a moment when I saw her. Her hair was longer and highlighted. This was a different Jordan. She looked sexier and more womanly. As usual, she had on her signature jacket. This time it was tan.

"Makeover?"

She touched her hair. "No, I just decided to change my look." She complimented me on my new Jil Sander suit.

"So, how are you?" she said. I told her about some of my new clients.

"I'm off to London tomorrow, staying at Thomas's place," she said. "He's coming here again." She smiled seductively.

"Tell him not to call me."

"Why, because he's married?"

"Isn't that enough of a reason?"

"I don't know," she said. "I could never figure men out, but fortunately, I don't have to." She told me about Caroline the Second, as I called her, and how they were now living together. She took a sip of Retsina. "Have you seen Luke?"

"I was out at his place almost a month ago," I said, trying not to give anything away. "Not since."

She sat and stared at me for a minute without saying anything. "And you haven't heard from him?"

I shook my head. "No."

"He's not easy to love."

I looked at her curiously. "What do you mean?"

"The limp," she said. "He's got this stupid complex because of it."

"I don't understand."

"When he was seven years old, his older sister shot him."

I looked at her in disbelief. "Oh God, why?"

"It wasn't on purpose," she shook her head. "Their father kept a gun in the house for protection—they were living in the Midwest at the time—and somehow she got hold of it. They were playing with it, whatever, and it went off suddenly and Luke was shot in the hip."

"How awful." I fixated on a child enduring the pain from something as inexplicable as a family gun going off because it was in another child's hand. How did he endure it? Maybe that explained the perpetually wounded quality about him. The shyness, the reticence, whatever it was. I flashed back to Laura and all the time she had to spend in the hospital alone, different from other kids who were outside, playing, living life the way children were supposed to.

"It was a deep wound, but it healed," Jordan said. "He was lucky not to have suffered any organ damage, but he was never able to walk completely straight after that and because of it, kids didn't treat him the same," she said. "You know how kids always manage to seize upon your weaknesses and play on them so they can get over on you and make you feel inferior?"

I nodded. Suddenly my whole picture of Luke seemed to come into focus. No wonder he was a loner.

"He was one of four kids and after that everyone teased him, including the kids in his own family when they wanted to get back at him for something." She stopped and spread butter on a slice of bread. "So, no surprise, he began to think of himself as the runt of the litter. Painting was his escape from it all, and from everyone. He used to go behind the house, into the woods, and spend hours there, no matter what the weather was."

"How do you know so much about him? I got the impression he didn't talk about himself very much."

"I've known him for a long time. It just came out."

I looked back at her warily and put down my fork.

Suddenly I had no interest in eating. Neither of us said anything and there was a long, strained silence. "Why are you telling me this?" I asked, finally looking directly at her.

She shrugged. "So you can understand him."

"You sure seem to…you know a lot about him." I sipped the wine and touched her arm. "How many kids in your family?" I asked, slowly.

She cut off a piece of lamb and ate it, then she put her fork down and turned to me. "Four," she said, nodding. Her smile disappeared as she turned to me. "I'm his half sister."

I stared back at Jordan. So now it all came clear. Yet whenever she spoke about him, I sensed that there was a distance between them.

"Are you close?"

"In some ways," she said. She made it sound mysterious. "But I can be competitive…and he doesn't like that." She laughed. "Especially when I win."

Every time I spoke to Jordan I felt as though she didn't answer questions, she just raised new ones. I looked at her questioningly, but suddenly she looked down at her watch. "Christ," she said, "it's almost two and I've got a meeting I forgot all about. We'll talk some other time," she said. "And I'll tell you about the woman, the one who came between us, okay?"

I tilted my head toward her, questioningly. Something about Jordan made me uneasy. I wanted to like her, but deep down, I didn't trust her. Maybe Luke felt the same way.

chapter twenty-four

I came home with the right size dog collar and a migraine. I took two Excedrin, and then two more. I rarely got headaches, so I didn't know whether the Retsina was to blame, the story about Luke, or her last words about the woman. Before I got into bed I called Arnie and asked if he wouldn't mind taking Harry out. When I opened the door he just stared.

"Christ, Sage, you look like crap."

"You're very kind. Thanks, Arnie, thanks a lot."

"No, I just mean, is there something I can do for you other than walking Harry?"

"Other than a frontal lobotomy, no." I got into bed after they left and must have dozed off because I was startled by the sound of knocking. I got out of bed and went to the door. Arnie had Harry's leash in one hand and the other held a plastic container. He held it out to me. "Chicken soup."

I looked at him and just about broke down. "Thanks Arnie," I sniveled. "I didn't mean to be so nasty to you before; I'm so sorry."

When you felt your most vulnerable, as if only a very fine membrane was protecting your sanity, the least bit of human decency could unhinge you.

"Sage, are you okay?"

"I just have to sleep. But thanks for the soup…and for Harry."

"Brie's coming over for dinner," he said, "but I guess you'll meet her another time."

• • •

I opened my eyes in the morning and I was flooded with a sense that something was different. Then it dawned on me. The headache was gone. The waters had parted and I was being given a chance at a new life. I called Mary Alice, who had called me a couple of days earlier.

"Do you want to come visit? We can go and get lobsters."

I didn't need persuading.

We hadn't seen each other since our last outing to the stores. She was running now instead of doing yoga. "I try to do a couple of miles every morning on the beach," she said. "I never would have imagined I would get into it, but it's so exhilarating, and I figure things out when I run."

Mary Alice was wearing workout pants and a sweatshirt. Her whole being looked softer and more comfortable now, as if she had turned into someone more sensual. We walked along the beach and talked about the weekend.

"I'm having a little dinner tomorrow night and I invited someone," she said, with a glint in her eye, "someone I want you to meet."

"Who?" I asked, cautiously. Almost involuntarily I

fixated on the date with Jim.

"Actually, he's one of the architects who worked on this house," she said. "He lives in town, and we just happened to run into each other at the gas station. We've had dinner a couple of times, and I enjoyed myself." She said it with a sense of surprise.

"Great," I said, both relieved and embarrassed. She was talking about her own life, not mine. "I can't wait to meet him."

"And there's another surprise," Mary Alice said. "I'm going to do a little taste testing. I've been working on some recipes, so we'll start out with some hors d'oeuvres and you can tell me what you think."

On our way back to the house I stopped when I saw something glittering in the sand—maybe just a tiny flickering of mica, but I knelt down to see what it was. I pushed away the sand. It was a man's gold wristwatch. I held it out to Mary Alice. "Is this yours?"

"Never seen it," she said. I picked it up and brushed away the sand that was covering the face. The glass was scratched and the expandable band was stretched out, but despite getting a beating from the natural world, it still kept perfect time.

• • •

We started dinner and then sat on the couch by the fireplace. Mary Alice was the only woman I knew who was an expert at lighting a fire. She piled up the wood carefully, added kindling, and lit a long match. It flared up impressively, as if responding to her hand. When she was satisfied with the flames, she sat back on the couch and turned to me.

"How's Luke?"

I told her about my lunch with Jordan. When I stopped and stared into the fire, she folded her arms across her chest. "People all have these internal lives, you never suspect how much baggage we all carry around."

"Is he up to date on his rent?"

"Not only is he up to date, he dropped by a few weeks ago and asked me if at some time in the future I'd consider selling him the land."

"What did you tell him?"

"I said I didn't know." She paused as if she were thinking about it. "The house has a few acres with it. My guess is he doesn't know how expensive it really is."

"Interest in his work seems to be booming; I guess he can thank his femme fatale agent for that." She looked at me curiously.

"I think he's sleeping with her."

"Why?"

I told her about the rumors, her body language, and then the tea.

"So what if he is? You're not."

"No...I have no claims on him. Anyway, he hasn't shown any interest in me—except as a part of his still life."

"You should see him again," she said, matter-of-factly, getting up to stoke the fire. "You have to go after what you want in life. It doesn't come to you."

"I don't know what I want."

"Well, see him again and find out."

chapter twenty-five

I woke to the sound of cooing doves. I showered and dressed and when I went downstairs, coffee was waiting. I spotted Mary Alice running along the beach, so I went out and waved. She gestured with her arm for me to join her. I made a face.

"No excuses," she shouted.

I grabbed a scarf and a down vest from the closet and went outside, running to catch up with her. I tried to keep pace, but I was barefoot, and eventually fell behind. It felt like twenty degrees with a biting wind. Still I ran along, warming up, eventually ready to beat my breast and yell out because it felt so good to do something hard. I went about half a mile, and then turned back and walked the rest of the way. My blood tingled as if I'd had a massage on the inside.

Mary Alice made me a stack of pancakes. "Think of all the extra calories you can eat now." She had clear, perfect skin, now the pink of perfect health.

"Why don't mine taste this good?" I said. I went over to

the counter to see what she put into the mix.

She grinned. "Hunger is the best cook. Other than that it's the vanilla, and the cinnamon-sugar."

I suspected there was a secret ingredient she wasn't telling me about, a clear case of the family recipe that didn't taste exactly the same when it was prepared by a member of another generation. Maybe Mary Alice was thinking of adding pancake mix to her product line.

We shopped in East Hampton after breakfast, starting out at antique stores that had hooked rugs and painted country furniture, then moving on to boutiques. Like Calypso St. Barth, where I bought pink jeans and a black ribbed cashmere sweater to wear over them. Then we went to Scoop, BCBG, and finally Tina the Store in Amagansett, to check out the great Wendy Nichol bags, the shoes, and the home design stuff with a modern Finnish vibe. The only shop we missed was a toy store. Mary Alice seemed happy just to look.

She shooed me out of the kitchen when we got back, but before I left I asked her about her architect friend.

"His name is Porter. Porter Huxley."

"God, how blue blood. Tell me he went to Yale."

"Princeton," she batted her eyelashes comically. "But he's not uppity, I swear." She pulled a large plastic bag filled with field greens out of the refrigerator and emptied it into a salad spinner. "I haven't had people over informally like this in I can't remember. So just take a hot bath and look gorgeous and leave everything to me."

Before I went upstairs to change I called Arnie to check on Harry. They took him to the park, Arnie said. He assured me that he and Brie were taking good care of him, and that gave me a twinge. Now even Arnie, my fallback, was a *we*. I stayed upstairs reading, glancing outside to watch the way the light changed on the water as it got closer to sunset. I couldn't imagine ever taking the view for granted. If I didn't have to be close to clients and the stores, it wouldn't take much to lure me to this kind of life.

Mary Alice was in the kitchen when I went down at 7:20. Porter was due any minute. I passed the dining table and stopped. I had set the table for her before I went upstairs, and had put out three place settings. Now there were four.

"Who else is coming?" She turned off the water and dried her hands, turning to me.

"Luke. I hope you don't mind."

"*What?*"

"I needed more taste testers—and anyway," she shrugged, nonchalantly, "he's out there by himself, so I thought he might like to be with people for a change."

"Oh my God, this is just SO embarrassing. This is… this is…" I was tongue-tied; that was super. "I'm just not psyched up to see him." I squeezed my eyes shut. "This is so blatant—such an obvious setup, Mary Alice. He'll think I masterminded this with you. I'm going upstairs. I am physically ill. Tell him I went to bed."

"You tell him," she said, walking out of the kitchen. "Because he just pulled up." As if a gun had gone off, the dogs bolted from their beds near the fireplace and shot across the living room, barking wildly. Almost simultaneously, a navy-blue Porsche came to a halt in the driveway.

I closed my eyes and for thirty seconds worked at a deep breathing exercise to center myself. When that failed I switched to *Shit, shit, shit, double shit, oh God, Mary Alice.* She ignored me and headed to the door. She kissed Porter and smiled at Luke, taking his hand. He walked in and looked at her almost sheepishly, then he saw me.

"Sage?" He made no attempt to hide his surprise.

"Luke—this is a surprise for me too; I didn't know you were coming."

Porter was close to fifty. He was tall and athletic looking, wearing small tortoiseshell glasses and a gray tweed jacket over a cranberry button-down shirt. There was an immediate warmth about him. He shook my hand and smiled. "Mary Alice has told me a lot about you."

"Not all bad, I hope."

He smiled. "She said you were a good friend."

Mary Alice carried in a tray with glasses and two bottles of wine. I followed her back into the kitchen as Porter talked to Luke.

"Give me something to do with my hands." She filled them with a platter filled with small slivers of steak wrapped around toothpicks, and another holding two clear glass pots of sauce.

"Bring these inside. These are for the first taste test."

I did as I was told, putting them down on the cocktail table. "I think we've got to wait until everything's set up to dig in. We'll be tasting Mary Alice's recipes."

Luke smiled and didn't say anything. Even when I turned, I knew his eyes were following me. Maybe it was being in the same house with him again, but I started thinking about the light in the room, wondering how I looked. Because Mary Alice thought of everything, the living room had soft, indirect lighting. In addition to the table lamps and wall sconces, there were thick white candles on the mantel as well as on the mirrored cocktail table. She came in after me, carrying a tray with more platters. Soon the table was covered with food and sauces.

I glanced at Luke. Worn jeans, Harley boots, and a dark green turtleneck sweater that fit snugly. He caught my eye and I looked away.

"Here's how it works," Mary Alice explained, almost flirtatiously. "First you taste the meat with the horseradish sauces and you rate them one to ten. Then you taste the fish with the mayonnaise sauces. Same: one to ten. The last thing I'll bring out is a barbecue sauce." She went back into the kitchen and came back with another bowl.

"It looks too good to touch," Luke joked. "Can I do some quick sketches?"

I gave him a withering glance. "This is about Mary Alice."

He held up his hands.

Porter smiled at me. "Why don't you start?"

I speared a piece of beef and dipped it in the first sauce. "Mmm."

"You're influencing the jury," Luke retaliated.

"Sorry, strike that." I jotted down my rating. We went back and forth without talking. I tried to surreptitiously steal a glance at Luke's paper to see how he was rating the sauces, but he cleared his throat and like an A student hiding his work from someone failing, he moved it so I couldn't see. Finally, we gave our sheets to Mary Alice.

"Don't bother with dinner, we're all full," I said.

"You can't be," she said. After we cleared away the small plates, she carried out a giant platter of spaghetti with shrimp, clams, oysters, and mussels, and we moved to the dining table. She seated Porter at the head of the table.

"Tell us about the houses you're working on," Mary Alice said.

"One of them is on the North Fork of Long Island," he said, "and the other is a ranch house in the Texas hill country."

"The locations are so different, isn't it hard to switch gears?" I said.

"Not as long as you're comfortable and familiar with the terrain," he said. "The design has to be organic. It has to be a product of the place you're in." For the Texas house, he said he was using local materials like corrugated metals, cattle fencing, and oil-field pipe in simple designs that worked with the landscape and the client's budget while offering shelter from the intense summer heat.

"You'd love the house," Mary Alice said. She turned to Porter. "I wish you had the pictures to show them."

"What does your own house look like?" Luke said.

"It's a simple saltbox, open to the sea. Bright, very spare. I'm a minimalist." Luke looked up as if Porter had just described his dream house.

"Where do you work?" he asked Luke.

Luke told him about the house and the grounds around it.

"I've driven past it," Porter said. "Great piece of property."

Luke scratched the back of his head and then smiled. "I'd like to buy it, but I don't know if Mary Alice is going to part with it, or if I'll ever be able to afford it."

Mary Alice was about to answer when her phone rang. She excused herself and went into the kitchen to take the call. She was back moments later.

"My friend in town pulled out her back...I'm just so sorry to do this, but I have to go over there. She's on the floor, she can barely get up. The timing is so bad, just when we're in the middle of dinner and you're all here." She looked genuinely upset.

"I'll drive you," Porter said.

"Absolutely not...I'll just—oh, my car," Mary Alice said. "I'll have to take you up on it, it's in the shop."

"Fine," he said, getting up.

She turned to me. "There's tiramisu in the refrigerator, please enjoy it."

"Can I do anything? I'll go with you, maybe there's something—"

She held up her hand. "No, please, enjoy the dessert; I'll be back as soon as I possibly can."

They rushed out and there we were. As if it wasn't uncomfortable enough that she had invited both of us, Luke and I were now face-to-face in an empty house. I glanced at him and then turned away. He sat there watching me, as if he were waiting to take his cue from me. He didn't seem nervous or uncomfortable, just uncertain.

We sat there, silently, finishing what was left on our plates. After my last forkful, I stood and, like a Stepford wife, started carrying plates into the kitchen.

"At least we can clean up for her." Without a word, Luke began piling plates on a tray and then carried it to the kitchen counter. I loaded the dishwasher, then washed the crystal while he dried. That absurd old expression, "Idle hands are the devil's workshop," came to mind and I almost laughed out loud. Was it the wine? I felt like a giddy fool. I turned toward the dishwasher so Luke couldn't see my stupid grin.

It was too ridiculous to try to explain.

"About that tiramisu," he said, finally.

"I forgot all about it." Most people ate when they were nervous; I completely lost interest in food. "Should we have it outside? There's a wonderful place to sit near the water." Mary Alice had what I can only describe as a lean-to, a wooden shelter with an open side facing the ocean. It was built into the sand. There was a bench inside where in winter you could curl up under a blanket and watch the sun setting while being sheltered from the wind. In summer, it protected you from the sun. It was a perfect spot to read. The inspiration for it, she told me, was a lean-to built high on a rock overlooking the water at The Point, a former Rockefeller estate, now an exclusive resort in the Adirondacks that gave out its location only after visitors made their reservations.

I put on my jacket and we carried coffee and tiramisu out there. There were matches on the side of the bench and two candles—I lit them.

"Amazing," Luke said, sitting back and looking out.

"Yes, except her life wasn't always the stuff of fantasies."

"How well do you know her?"

"I worked with her on her wardrobe a few months ago. We became good friends after that."

"So you go shopping for people and put their wardrobes together?"

"Yes."

He narrowed his eyes. "What would you tell me to buy?"

I leaned back and studied him. Only then did I realize I hadn't thought much about his clothes—except for the jacket he wore at his gallery opening. It was because he instinctively wore what belonged on him. I imagined he picked clothes with the same subtle instinct that he picked colors for his paintings.

"I wouldn't change anything," I said. "What you wear looks good on you. I like the worn jeans, T-shirts. I like you in black with your blond hair, but you look good in colors too—purple, turquoise, navy. You're outdoors most of the time. You need clothes that are comfortable. You don't need eight-hundred-dollar gabardine pants."

"That's a relief. I can continue shopping at the thrift shop. And what about you? Do you spend a lot of time thinking about what you put on?"

"It depends on where I'm going." I hoped he wouldn't ask how much time I spent orchestrating the outfit that I wore to his opening. "Clothes are fun and for me they're kind of an art form. You think a lot about what colors you use, right?" He nodded. "It's the same thing." I took a forkful of tiramisu and then a sip of coffee.

"Did you think about what you were going to wear tonight?" he asked.

"I didn't know you were going to be here."

"What would you have worn if you did?"

"Just this." I pointed to my outfit. "I bought these in town today; I liked the color."

"I liked the rose," Luke said, reaching over and wiping away a crumb on the side of my mouth with his finger. "I kept thinking about that."

I swallowed, involuntarily. "It was just an accessory." It came out so low that I was sure he couldn't hear me. He took the coffee out of my hand and leaned over, pulling me toward him by gripping the sides of the blanket that was around my shoulders. Our faces were only inches apart and then he pressed his forehead against mine, closing his eyes. It felt as though he were inhaling my closeness as he took in a breath in a heavy, almost labored way, then he began to pull back. I slipped my hand behind his neck and stopped him from moving, pressing my lips against his. He leaned into me, kissing me softly at first and then harder, finally pushing me against the back of the bench. I reached my hand up the back of his hair, tugging on it.

"Why didn't you come back again?" he whispered, imploringly. "I waited for you."

I caught my breath. "You could have called. I didn't feel like a model, I felt like an object you were sketching."

"I get so intense when I work. You don't know me," he said. "It wasn't going right, I was frustrated." He pulled the blanket away and slid my sweater up, tracing his fingers lightly over the length of my ribs as if he were trying to commit the feel of them to memory. He unbuttoned my jeans, and I pulled back.

"Let's go inside."

He took my hand and we walked toward the house. I led him up to my room and opened the door. Luke stood there, taking it all in. "I didn't know people really lived like this."

I closed the door and he leaned against me, pinning me to the back of it. If there was awkwardness before, his physical closeness literally eliminated any strange distance between us. No more tension, no inhibitions. He scooped up my hair and found my neck, running his lips down the side of it. With one hand, he unzipped my jeans and tugged them down gently to the floor. He stared at the pink lace La Perla eyelet underwear I had on, and he stopped.

"Do you always wear things like that?" he asked, almost

breathless, as if it hurt to talk.

"I like underwear," I whispered. "Don't you?"

He laughed, nodding his head slowly as he slid off the panties. He held them out to study them. "All these surprises."

Luke was tight and lean like an athlete, almost underfed, with square shoulders and small hips. He unbuttoned his jeans and pushed them to the floor. That's when I saw the scar. He saw that I noticed, but didn't say anything as he led me to the bed and we fell back onto it.

He made love the same way he painted, with total absorption, consumed by passion, almost to the point of being in pain. I felt like an unformed piece of clay he needed to see and feel to understand before he worked on it. It was only in bed that I saw the playful side of him. He was released from himself and the emotions I sensed were so restrained in him came through. We kissed, played, fought, rolled over each other so that he was over me, then I was over him, and finally he was on top again, almost sitting up. Finally, he slid down, thrusting himself inside of me, making me forget everything else in the world except him and the feel of him inside me.

We lay next to each other without speaking when it was over. I put an arm over his chest and he took my hand and kissed it. I was about to close my eyes when he sat up and kissed my breast, surprising me by suddenly sucking the skin, fixating on a tiny patch where the tattoo had been.

"That's exactly where it was," he said. He looked at me with a self-satisfied grin. "I've tattooed you again." I threw back my head, almost unable to speak.

"Yes," I said. "You have."

chapter twenty-six

I made us scrambled eggs and smoked salmon for breakfast, and carried it upstairs so we could eat in bed.

"This is amazing," he said, taking the plate from me. He took a forkful and fed the next one to me. "What are you doing today?" he asked.

"Hanging out here for a while and then heading back to the city. What about you?"

"Working. A client of Kyla's in Italy is interested in buying a few new things and she's going to send him some slides as soon as I finish the new ones."

"So now you're eating?"

He nodded, taking another forkful of eggs. "I'm also losing my freedom. People who are interested in your work want to meet you." He made a face.

"But you don't want to meet them?"

"I don't care."

"Maybe they want a little piece of you," I teased.

"I don't have much to give," he said, looking at me

almost guiltily.

"I doubt that," I said, ignoring the subtext.

"It's true."

I focused instead on what I was feeling. In the full sunlight of the room, his eyes were, sea green, his blond hair hanging loosely on the sides of a face lightly shadowed by a dark beard. I ached with desire for him. I leaned toward him and he took me into his arms.

"The problem with beautiful women is they're habit forming," he whispered in my ear, making me shiver. "You need to have them around all the time and keep looking at them in the changing light. It makes it very, very hard to concentrate."

"Could you work with me around?"

"You'd be a distraction," he said, lifting a handful of my hair, studying it as it fell away, little by little. Then he was on top of me and inside me, and all I remember thinking was that everything about us being together felt so right.

• • •

I don't remember hearing Mary Alice come in, and when we dressed and went downstairs, her bedroom door was still closed. There was a Post-it on it: "Sage, got in early this morning. I'll catch up with you this evening when you're home. Thanks for cleaning up!"

• • •

We went back to Luke's and on the way we stopped in town to buy food for a late lunch. We spread a blanket outside and set out the food. It looked as though it had been art directed for a still life: Fried chicken, salad, fruit, and wine. I was wearing a down jacket and gloves, reluctantly taking them off to eat the chicken. Luke found it amusing. He seemed oblivious to the cold. All he had on was his turtleneck sweater and jeans. After we finished, we stared up at the sky, watching the sun go down. The property was about four acres, and from the house you couldn't see any others. The outdoors made him feel safe, he said.

"Do you do this all the time?"

He hesitated, as if talking didn't come naturally to him. Maybe he was out of practice. "I'm outside all the time," he said, in a halting voice. "But not to picnic—not like this. You're the first." He stared off, as if he were looking back into his past, and his face turned serious. "I really grew up outside." I reached over and pushed a lock of hair away from his eye. He took my hand and squeezed it. "Stay here tonight. Don't leave, please." He looked at me quizzically, his face flickering with a million conflicting emotions.

"I have to be back early in the morning for work, I can't."

He lay back on the blanket and closed his eyes. Finally, he turned his face toward me. "Do you really change people's lives?"

"When you change someone's clothes and how they look to themselves and other people, you give them a license to be someone else, someone better and more confident. You know what a difference the right color or shape makes, whether it's on someone or on a canvas."

"You know what Jackson Pollock said?" he asked.

"What?"

"It's all a big game of construction, some with a brush, some with a shovel, some choose a pen."

"There's a need to create," I said, "or is it propagate?"

He looked back at me and I saw that distance again. "When are you going to sit for me again?"

"I don't know," I said, getting to my feet as a thought took hold of me that gave me a queasy feeling. Would our relationship be over when he finished the painting? Would he find some other muse? We went inside and he lit a fire. He sat in front of it and even though I knew I had to go, I joined him. Almost instinctively, we started undressing each other. My sweater, his. My jeans, then his, until the slow dance of undressing was over and we were together, in front of the fire with the heat on our backs. I should have been thinking about making love to him, but instead I was dreading the fact that I had to leave. I turned to him and ran my hand down the length of his body, and over the terrible white knotted scar on his hip.

"Does it hurt?"

He squeezed his eyes shut momentarily. "Just in my head."

He saw the questioning look in my eyes. "Another time," he said, putting up the wall. I got up slowly and started to dress. "I've got a long drive." He stood up and drew me to him. Several minutes went by and neither of us moved.

"Goodbye, Sage," he whispered.

chapter twenty-seven

A lot of my work was about pain. One of my clients had alopecia areata and had lost most of her hair. Much of our time was spent searching for flattering hats and scarves so she felt comfortable.

"I want to look chic," she said, "not bald."

She didn't talk much about the condition, but I hoped that if she needed to, she'd feel close enough to me to open up. But she couldn't hide the pain, not all the time. It showed in her face for brief moments when we shopped and we couldn't find exactly what we needed. There were flashes of darkness, and isolation or resigned frowns.

At the end of our outing, though, we managed to find just the right oversized straw hats for summer in different colors to match her oufits, and for winter a few fur hats as well as crocheted hats with crocheted roses. "My props," she called them.

I watched her try them on in her apartment, along with the outfits we bought to go with them. She exhaled loudly.

"This works," she said, nodding. "I have my confidence back." The corners of her mouth turned up slightly as she studied herself in the mirror.

"Then it will show," I said, "inside and out."

I have my confidence back. Offhand remarks like that from clients made me feel there was a reason for me to get up in the morning. It wasn't about the clothes. It was about the person wearing them, and the fact that I had given them something intangible and more important than the dress or the accessory.

Another client wore an insulin pump, so we had to find the right pants or skirts and the jackets or cardigans to cover and hide it. I knew how hard it was for her, but I also saw a woman who made a conscious decision not to dwell on what she couldn't change. So we talked about everything but diabetes and the way she was forced to minister to it every day, even though neither of us ever forgot that. Sometimes she said things like, "If this is the worst thing…" and then she waved it away and we talked about something else.

Even if someone didn't have a condition with a name, every one of us lived with varying amounts of pain and disappointment. The more experiences I had in my own life, the more I could empathize.

Some people didn't dignify what they saw as their shortcomings by giving in to them. Instead, they built on what was right about their bodies, faces, and minds and shored themselves up. My job was to be their cheerleader, armed with the tools to make them look their best. As Greta Garbo said, "Darling, the legs aren't so beautiful. I just know what to do with them."

I haven't met many people who don't have something to

hide, or shift the focus away from, and there is always a way.

My week started out with a client I worked with for three years in a row, starting when she was just out of college. She was like no other. She didn't need a wardrobe consultant, she needed a shrink. She was single, never married, and born in Sicily. Almost every year she went home for a visit, or at least contemplated going home, and that's where I came in. I bought her new clothes for the trip, packed the suitcase, and got it ready. I left it by the door, where it stood—three months ahead of time.

I usually have a good handle on my clients. By the time we've been together for many hours over the course of a week, a month, or often several years, I know about their families, their jobs, their pets, their feelings about themselves, and their attitudes about clothes. But Maria Elena was a mystery. Her secrets were packed up in her bag along with her wishes, her dreams, and her phobias. I didn't ask about her family and she didn't tell me. She once said she didn't work, but she never told me what she did instead. I knew she didn't have a husband, or children, unless they were in Italy. So I did the job that she asked me to do, and I left the suitcase ready. The following year she never told me whether she made the trip or didn't.

This time when I left her apartment, I glanced back at the suitcase as I approached the door. Her private world reminded me of Luke's and how I had walked out of his life, a life I also knew very little about.

• • •

Arnie phoned a week after I got back from Mary Alice's. He wanted to have dinner.

"I found a pretty decent Greek joint that delivers. You up for it?" He came in with a bottle of wine, and I uncorked it. It had been weeks since we got together. I'm not sure whether it was the advice I gave him, but he was wearing a cocoa-brown shirt and chocolate-brown pants, a vast improvement over some of the get-ups I'd seen him in.

"Lookin' good." I high-fived him.

"Thanks."

"So how's Brie?" I said as I scrubbed out Harry's bowl and refilled it.

"Uh, okay."

I put the bowl down and Harry just about inhaled the food. If you turned away to wash a glass while he was eating, when you looked back all the food would be gone.

"Okay?"

"She had to go out of town on a business trip," he said. The doorman buzzed up at that moment and I went to the door.

"Are you seeing her exclusively or have you tried to meet other women?" I said, unpacking the moussaka and a large Greek salad. I suppose I was obsessed with the idea of fidelity.

"The online thing didn't work out."

"Oh, how come?"

"You're bombarded with all these women and after a while you forget who said what when you have, like, four people you're talking to. I thought I was having a conversation with a Wall Street lawyer, and then I realized she was someone else and I was talking to a waitress in

Jersey. It's not my style."

"But Brie is?"

"No…I thought so in the beginning, but now I think we're better off being friends."

"Did anything happen?"

He shrugged and stared at the floor. I studied Arnie, not sure how hard I should push.

"I see," I said, even though I didn't. "I'm sorry I didn't meet her; you acted like you really liked her, so I was anxious to see what she was like."

Arnie stared at me and then looked away, fixated on the fascinating tip of his shoe. "It turned out she was having an affair with her boss," he said, looking back at me. "She liked me as a friend."

"I'm sorry, Arnie," I reached out and squeezed his shoulder. "I really am."

He pulled back and raised his chin. "There are a lot of fish."

"Yes there are." I was tempted to add, because I was in a sour mood, *but a lot of them are rotten.*

chapter twenty-eight

After I found Harry in a shelter in Queens—and I thought of him as my thank-you gift for helping—I began volunteering at different places once or twice a month. One Sunday we planted trees in Central Park. Another time we helped pick up trash after a parade.

But my favorite times were my afternoons or evenings with Laura. Was she like the child I hoped to have one day? Maybe. But whatever it was, I felt a closeness to her I had never felt with anyone before, not counting Harry.

I often told her about him because she said she loved dogs, and she listened, fascinated. If I ever found out how to have him assessed so he passed what they called the Good Citizen test, I promised to bring him with me, and the idea thrilled her. When I wasn't talking about Harry or books, I went on endlessly about clothes because they were my life, or most of it, and even though you'd imagine that what you wore and how you looked in clothes was probably the furthest thing from the life of a kid in a hospital, she was always riveted.

"I love your clothes," she said, complimenting me the way she always did. And then she told me again about the blue dress she wore for her birthday. It was made of satin and it had a big navy-blue velvet sash that went around her waist.

"Blue? I love blue," I said. "Especially navy. When's your birthday?"

"In eight weeks."

"I'll buy you a dress," I said, "the prettiest dress in the whole world."

"Really?"

"Really!"

When it was time for me to go, I gave Laura a hug. "See you in two weeks." She gave me a thumbs-up. I walked out of the unit, passing nurses in white cotton jackets. Everyone seemed lost in work. Up at the main desk, there were bouquets of flowers waiting to be delivered. An open box of cookies was on the reception desk, probably left by a grateful parent.

I waited a long time for the elevator and finally rode down with a crowd of people, all of us going through the giant revolving door that led to the street. We left behind the well-lit corridors with the medicinal smells, and went out into the fresh night air and the world of the lucky. I walked to the bus stop and tilted my head up to the black sky.

"Please, please," I whispered, pressing my fingers hard to my mouth. "You know I don't ask much—but please, now please...just this."

chapter twenty-nine

Not that I kept track of these things precisely, but three weeks, one day, and seven hours had gone by and I hadn't heard from Luke. I refused to accept that it was a one night/two-day stand, but the more time that passed, the more I began to think of our lovemaking—perhaps that word was an overstatement—that way.

Was it me? Was I such a truly terrible judge of character? Was I unable to discern how someone felt about me? Was I a quick sexual fix to juice him up before he went back to being a fuck-up so he would continue to fail at relationships, keeping women at bay for his own safety? Maybe he really did have very little to give anyone. Why didn't women believe men who told them things like that?

I sat and stared at the phone. I lifted the receiver. I whispered Luke's name and waited. But no miraculous connection was established. There was no one on the other end. Slowly, over the next days and then weeks, the hurt turned to anger. I imagined sneaking into the gallery that displayed his work and spray-painting one of his canvases. *SELFISH SHIT*. Then I'd slip out as quietly as I had come in. The way the media was these days, though, the publicity would probably help him. The story would get press attention, someone would raise questions as to whether he himself was behind it, and in the process someone would discover he was a talented painter.

· · ·

I arranged to meet Mary Alice for lunch at Balthazar, an appealing replica of a Parisian bistro on Spring Street in Soho. I ordered a salad with warm goat cheese and a caramelized onion tart. She had braised short ribs. We shared the crusty French bread while we waited.

"How's your sick friend—the one with the bad back?" I said as I slathered the bread with too much butter, something Mary Alice didn't miss. Even though I'd spoken to her a couple of times since my visit, we hadn't gotten together.

"Oh, fine now," she said, waving her hand to the side. She absentmindedly twisted one of the sapphire stack rings on her finger around and around, a nervous gesture I hadn't seen her do, at least not since the first time I met her. I could have sworn she said her friend had herniated disks and was almost bedridden, contemplating risky surgery. How had she recovered so quickly?

"Oh my GOD," I said, as I leaned all the way across the table when it hit me. "You didn't." I shook my head in disbelief. "I am soooo dumb—I fell for it."

She looked back at me, confused. "Didn't what, and why are you so dumb?"

"The sick friend business. It took me this long to realize." I drummed my fingers on the table. "You faked the whole thing. I don't know how it didn't hit me until just now."

"*Sage*," she said, outraged, as if I had it all wrong. She looked away arrogantly and we sat there, not speaking. A moment later she bit her bottom lip and her face broke into a smile. "I wondered when you'd realize." Several seconds went by. "If I hadn't done it, when would you have gone to see him again? Life is short, you have to seize the moment."

"A lot of good it did me," I snapped back. A model type walked by the window in a camel-colored cashmere Calvin Klein coat. I peered out to see what kind of boots she had on.

"I know," she said, sympathetically. "That was just so lousy." She grimaced. "Men can be such a pain in the ass."

"Pain in the ass? He's a dysfunctional human being. He goes back into that shell of his and hibernates or something."

She studied me intently and didn't say anything.

"What?"

"He called me this morning," she said, softening.

"What did he say?"

"You're not going to like it."

"What?" I asked, nauseous with anticipation.

"He moved to France."

I opened my mouth to speak, but nothing came out.

"Apparently there was a house in Vétheuil where Monet used to live and it became available for rent. He took it for six months or a year, I'm not sure."

"He's giving up *your* house?"

"No, that's why he called. He said he'd be wiring me the money for the rent. He wants to keep the place and he asked if I could go over there occasionally and pick up his mail."

"Maybe I should be his landlord. You're the only one he feels the need to keep in touch with." Out the window I saw a teenage boy walk by with his arm slung around the shoulder of a girl with long blonde hair, as if he had staked his claim on her. I looked away. "Well, now I can move on with my life. He's an ocean away communing with Monet's ghost." *Closure*, I thought to myself, although I despised that word.

"He left his address…do you want it?"

I shook my head back and forth deliberately.

"He asked about you," she said, almost singsong.

I looked up, surprised. "What did he say?"

"He wanted to know if I'd seen you." I looked at her and my eyes filmed over. Mary Alice was only about ten or twelve years older than me, but because of her strong personality I always felt as though she were a wise family member whom I could confide in. Now I wanted her shoulder. "He's not staying there forever. You could write, or call. " She shrugged. "Even go."

"A lot of women would crawl, but that's not me." I reached down and smoothed the soft white napkin that covered my lap. "Moving out without even saying a word?"

"He's difficult," she said, exasperated, "and I'm not telling you what to do, but I do know he probably makes a habit of disappointing people before they have a chance to disappoint him. Failure is his safety net—which is not to say he can't change."

"He's hard work—Jordan was right, and you know what? I'm tired." I paused and stared back out the window. I spent all day long, sometimes six days a week, trying to fix everyone else's bodies, egos, and minds. I didn't want to have to do therapy on my own relationships. "He's gone… it's better off."

When the food came we made small talk about other restaurants, the movies, and her plans for marketing her sauces. When she spoke about the business, she got lost in it. She didn't have to deal with other people and their distorted self-images. All she had to do was get them to spend a few dollars to try something new to titillate their palates. After lunch she had an appointment to meet with a group of people about setting up a commercial kitchen in a space in East Quogue, where the rents were a lot lower than in East Hampton.

She reached into her briefcase and pulled out a plastic sleeve that held a picture of a logo: three green bottles surrounded by quick line drawings of herbs and vegetables. There was a little sketch of a sun shining down on the word *Soupçon*.

"What do you think?"

"Wonderful," I said, excited for her. "It's so fresh, it's charming. I love the childlike feel."

"Luke did it," she said, before I had a chance to ask.

I fixated on the paper as a stabbing sadness spread over me.

"He wouldn't let me pay him," she said. "I think he's hoping that somewhere down the line, if he helps me design the graphics for the company, it'll go toward a down payment on the property."

"Will you sell it to him?"

She arched an eyebrow and shrugged. "He loves being there, and since I bought it for my mother and think of her every time I pass it, I like the idea of knowing that it's in the hands of someone who cares about it and sees it for its beauty. I know he won't put up condos. It was going to be my gift to her—open land that she could have all to herself. A refuge. She deserved that," she said, her voice cracking. "She would have loved the tranquility." She looked away. "She was a gardener and a bird watcher—she lived such a simple life."

"The way you think about land changes when you're outside the city," I said, as I realized it for the first time. "When you're in an apartment, all you think about is square footage. But every time I come to see you and we go food shopping, I see the plants and think of the seasons and I'm aware of the rhythms of life. I guess that's how most of the world lives—we're such an aberration."

"That's why when Richard and I separated, I picked the house," Mary Alice said. "You get into life's cycles and see your place in the universe. In Manhattan you're preoccupied with little annoyances like finding a cab or not getting to the theater on time. Things that shouldn't matter are a calamity. The whole city is in cardiac arrest." I saw that downcast look in her eyes again.

"I was just too late getting around to building on the land," she said, holding my gaze. "You can't waste time agonizing about life and the should-bes and the what-ifs. You have to go after what you want, Sage," she whispered. "And you have to do it now. It all can change in a minute."

I reached across the table and squeezed her hand. "I think I got the better part in our friendship. I've gained so much from you and you've been such a good friend."

"And you helped open my mind, by opening up my

closet," she said. "Recuperative wardrobe surgery, not to mention being there for me and helping me come out of my hardboiled shell."

"Can I get you some dessert?"

Why was it that waiters seemed to pride themselves on interrupting conversations when you were exchanging the most meaningful sentiments? Then again, maybe they instinctively knew when it was time for you to stop talking.

"This is no place to refuse dessert," Mary Alice said. We ordered fruit tarts and coffee and started talking about changes in Soho. Then I realized that I'd been so self-absorbed that I hadn't asked her about Porter. "How's that going?"

Her face lit up. "He's in Maine working on a house. He invited me to spend a long weekend up there with him. It's a house on a narrow peninsula called Orr's Island that faces a protected inlet of water, rather than the open ocean." I thought of my last trip to Maine and my day trip to Monhegan Island, a paradise for artists, probably best known as the place that three generations of Wyeths loved and painted.

"I like Porter," I said. "I think he's good for you."

"I admire the way he looks at the world," she said. "And it's not about making money."

"That's why he got along with Luke. They're both consumed by the natural world. They both have a vision."

"He was very taken with him," she said, even though I didn't ask. "He said he was surprised that he was as accessible as he was. 'No pretensions,' I think were his words."

He was right about that. Luke was himself. He didn't try to impress people. He was more interested in seeing than being seen. Everything around him interested him, particularly if it applied to his canvas.

• • •

When you spend so much of your time traveling around the city, you can't help running into people you know. Sometimes you met the same few people repeatedly, as if you were on the same life circuit. And sometimes it was just serendipitous when you crossed paths with someone totally unexpected. I walked west for a few blocks along Eighth Street over to University Place, near New York University. People on bicycles whizzed by. If you dared step into the street without looking, you risked your life. I held out my hand to get a cab going uptown. One pulled up, and out of nowhere, a man came forward and opened the door. I was ready to protest that he was stealing my cab. I pivoted, and we collided. "Excuse me," I said indignantly. I stepped back, and looked up to find that the man I had walked into was Thomas Martin. "My God, you're the last person that I expected to fight for a cab."

"Sage," he said, equally surprised.

"So which one of you is gettin' in?" the driver yelled as we stood there, while horns started to blast. "I'm blocking traffic."

"It's okay," I said, "take it, please."

"Never mind," he said, shooing the driver off. "So how have you been?"

Why was it that he always made me come unglued? "Good," I said, hastily. I hadn't thought about him in a long time. "Excellent."

He looked at me with a mocking smile. "You can call me Jordan if you'd rather."

I gave him a false laugh. "When did you get back?"

"Just a few days ago. Jordan and I switched this time." He looked at his watch. "Have a drink with me. I've got a dinner at eight, but we have forty-five minutes. What do you say?" I had told Jennelle that I'd be at her place at around seven thirty, but I knew she wouldn't mind.

We walked up University to Corkbuzz Wine Studio on Thirteenth Street, where the tables were bathed in a golden light. Déjà vu all over again. Wine on an empty stomach, blotto in no time. But he was rushing off to a dinner, so I didn't have to fear any invitations. Once again, he was impeccably dressed. A slate-gray suit, a dove-gray shirt, and a steely tie. I searched for some indicator of imperfection—a scuffed shoe, a missing button, a frayed cuff—but he was flawless. Did he pick out his own clothes or did his wife dress him? Probably bought his own stuff, otherwise he wouldn't quite know what to wear with what.

The bartender came over. I could have used a martini. "Coke," I said. He had beer. I looked over at him and couldn't resist glancing at his left hand. Still no band. This time he caught me.

"I'm separated," he said, as though anticipating my question.

"Oh…I'm sorry."

I thought of asking him what happened, but held back. It was none of my business.

"Funny, how life works," he said. "It turned out that she was the one having an affair. If I had only known," he said, staring off.

189

"How long were you married?"

"Eight years, but I suppose it was more like five if you count all the time that I was away."

"It's so much harder if one of you travels." A moment later it hit me that I was talking about my own life, too. I wondered what Thomas's wife looked like. Was she beautiful? He probably attracted legions of women; he could have his pick. Then again, so could Luke, and he was in France. Thomas stared off into the distance.

"What would you have done differently?"

He smiled enigmatically. "I would have cheated." I knew he was only half kidding. "Lord knows I had the opportunities." He waved his hand to the side. "But I had some kind of moral code, and obviously she didn't." I studied him and saw a vulnerability that hadn't been there before.

"Do you have children?"

"No. So it's a clean break."

"I'm sorry, Thomas, really."

"Now I can pursue beautiful, single women like Sage Parker—so there's a plus side to it."

"So tell me," I said, again feeling the need to steer the conversation away from where it was headed. "Have you seen Jordan, or do you just miss each other like ships passing in the night?"

"We talk on the phone," he said, "but we don't get a chance to see each other much although we sleep in each other's beds—or, I should say, we sleep in each other's guest rooms. She's actually a good friend of my wife's."

"How did you meet?" I realized for the first time I had never asked him.

"We met in London the summer after she graduated

from school. We started dating. That was before she realized she was gay—or who knows," he said, widening his eyes for effect, "maybe I had something to do with her realizing it."

"Nobody is who you think they are. It's taken me a while to find that out."

"We all have our mysteries," he said, and then he narrowed his eyes. "So what's yours?"

"I'm the exception. I'm very straightforward. No deception."

"You're a woman," he said, "so I doubt that."

"It's obvious you're going through your 'I hate women' stage. It'll pass."

He threw his head back and laughed. "Me, a misogynist? Never. I love women. The problem was I married too early, didn't sample enough of them." He leaned across the table and took my hand. "Why don't we go out for a real evening? French food, champagne. I'm free tomorrow, if you are."

"I'm seeing someone." I was about to add I *had* been, but decided not to.

He raised his eyebrows. "Who's the lucky guy, a fellow wardrobe person?"

"Funny. No, and actually, you might know him."

"Oh?" He hoisted his beer and stared at me as he tilted his head back and drank.

"Jordan's half brother, Luke."

"Hmmm," he said, true to form. "Bohemian type, starving artist." He shook his head. "I can afford to show you a much better time."

"How well do you know him?" I asked, ignoring that.

"Not well. We met only once, at her apartment. He was in the process of moving his stuff out of the city. There

191

was a girlfriend at the time, but I don't think it lasted all that long."

No surprise, but I didn't stop him.

"Jordan kept tabs on him," he said. "She used to help him pay the bills so he could keep painting. She felt responsible for him." He shrugged. "I haven't heard much about him in a long time."

"He's in France for a while, following in Monet's footsteps."

"So then you're free." He looked at me expectantly.

"No," I said, giving him a small smile. "I have some kind of moral code."

He glanced at his watch and motioned to the waiter for the check. "Don't make the mistake I did, Sage. Don't let life pass you by."

That was starting to sound familiar. We walked out to the street and he hailed a cab. He opened the door for me and I climbed in. "Goodbye, Sage," he said, closing the door.

chapter thirty

Jennelle was talking to a new artist on her cell as she waved me in. It wasn't an apartment anymore—it had become an office. She had hundreds of slides on the wall, of different artists' work. A wall that used to be bare was now covered with file cabinets.

"Two paintings aren't enough," she said, shaking her head. "I can't get a show for you based on two canvases." She went through a series of head bobs and then rolled her eyes to me. "I know you changed your style. So you have to build up a portfolio."

It sounded like she was talking the talk, but what did I know? Mine was a one-on-one business, and she had to sell her client to a gallery or an ad agency before they got a chance to prove themselves. Finally, she hung up.

"Hey, mogul."

"I'm turning off my cell," she said. "When you work from home, your workday never ends. The worst scenario is using your bedroom as your office so the first and last thing you see each morning and night is the computer. What's going on?"

"Guess who I just ran into?"

"I give up."

"Thomas, Thomas Martin. Remember the James Bond type who I thought was Jordan?"

"No way!"

"Way, and he told me he's separated."

"Probably a story."

"I don't think so. He sounded upset about it. Turned out his wife was cheating on him."

She looked at me and raised her eyebrows. "Would you leave your spouse if you found out he was sleeping with someone else?"

"I don't think it would endear me to him. What about you?"

"I'd like to think I could handle it," Jennelle said. "Assuming he swore that he wasn't seeing her any more or didn't want to. But I don't know."

"I imagine a lot of relationships that should have gone on ended abruptly because one of the partners turned away and a lot of good years together were just forgotten."

"That sounds rather idealistic," she said.

"Maybe, and I'd probably feel as though I'd been stabbed and could never trust the guy again," I said, curling up on her couch. "I think Luke sleeps with Kyla, but I guess that's different. We're not a couple. We're not anything." I shrugged. "I was a two-day stand—one notch above a one night."

"But he *is* coming back."

"Maybe."

"Have you spoken to him?"

"He doesn't know what a phone is."

"Call Thomas," Jennelle said. "He looks like James Bond, he's separated, and you're hesitating?"

"You know the crazy thing about very conventionally gorgeous men?"

"I give up."

"They're destined to disappoint you," I said.

"And why is that, Dr. Phil?"

"You start out so enamored of them it can only go downhill. Sooner or later you find out they're just normal human beings."

"You know what I think?" Jennelle asked.

I shook my head.

"I think that's bullshit. I think you're scared of him for some reason. Either that or you're just plain not interested in meeting anyone because you're pining away over Luke, who's a continent away and may never come back." She glared at me. "Then again, maybe that's safe."

I thought of all the expat American artists who made their homes in Europe. She was probably right.

We didn't discuss it any more, we ate. After the pizza we turned on Turner Classic Movies. "Please not *Last Year at Marienbad*, or another one of Greg's favorites."

Jennelle laughed. "You really have dated a lot of beauties."

"Your friend Jim notwithstanding." We looked through the guide to see what they were showing. "You're so lucky to have found Daniel. He's creative, not too abnormal, he has his own business, his art, a life, and he loves you."

She looked off into the distance.

"What?"

"I wasn't going to tell you," she said, "but he told me that before we started dating, he saw Kyla." She paused. "It didn't last very long, a couple of nights, I think, but it was bothering him when we started talking about Luke, and he wanted to get it off his chest."

"Who hasn't she slept with?"

"The answer to your next question is: he didn't say."

"I didn't ask."

"You were thinking about it," Jennelle said.

• • •

Monday morning at ten. I was still in bed reading the newspaper. No one knew I'd taken the morning off. I was rarely home then and clients always called on my cell. I considered letting the machine pick up. But when the ringing stopped, I had a sudden change of heart.

"Is this Sage? Sage Parker?" I didn't recognize her voice. I guessed it wasn't work-related. It was a tentative voice, a strained one.

"Yes?"

"My daughter told me a lot about you..." Her trancelike voice trailed off.

"I'm sorry, but...who's your daughter?"

"Laura," she said. "Laura Morgan, you read her stories—"

"Oh, yes."

"We knew it was coming," she said, her voice a monotone, "we just didn't think...so soon."

"Oh!" It came out as a cry. "I'm so sorry." I felt a stab

of pain inside me.

"The reason I'm calling," she said, drawing a breath, "is that she talked so much about you. She was so excited about your visits. And she told us about the dress and how on her birthday, you promised to bring her—" She stopped. "I don't even know if I should ask you...oh my God..." I waited while there was a stifled cry.

"Please, what?"

"A dress," she said, finally. "I'd like to buy her something very special, to wear for..."

You never fool anyone when you try to pretend that you're not choking back tears. Even if they're on the opposite end of the phone, they know. They can hear it in the silence. But I was embarrassed by the sudden avalanche of sadness that wanted to break out of me. "Can you excuse me just a minute?"

"Of course."

I went into the bathroom and buried my face in the towel. I let out one sob after another and then told myself it was enough. I couldn't do that, not to her mother. It was hard enough for her to pick up the phone and call me. I went back to the bedroom and picked up the phone.

"I'll find the dress for you," I said. "I'd be honored to."

chapter thirty-one

I spent the day shopping, but not for clothes for the CEO of an insurance company who needed new outfits, or for the criminal lawyer who wanted a few new elegant suits for an upcoming trial. I spent the day going to children's clothing stores like Jacadi, Adrian East, and Lester's, looking for the perfect dress for a perfect little girl who lived in an imperfect world, a world that wasn't fair.

Consumers perpetually complained about the lack of attention from salespeople in Manhattan stores. For me it was a relief not to have people asking me if I needed help. There was no way I could tell them how old she was, what size she wore, or worst of all, what the occasion was.

I looked through racks and racks of dresses, but I couldn't find what I was looking for. Nothing was magical enough. Nothing transported me. I wanted a dress an angel would wear. Finally I decided to make it myself. I went to Paron Fabrics on West 39th Street in the Garment District, where I found the perfect blush-pink silk and tiny pink silk roses to edge the sleeves and hem.

I learned to sew in high school. The first thing we made was a blouse. I bought a hideous mustard-color cotton with a small cranberry print. The pattern was simple: cap sleeves and a round neck. It was short, extending just a couple of inches below the waist. Of course, every time I lifted my arms, the entire blouse lifted with them. None of that mattered to my teacher, aptly named Mrs. Singer. Her only concern was that none of us put straight pins into our mouths. If we did, it was grounds for immediate failure.

Sewing was hard for me at first. It was tricky keeping the seams straight, and learning how to turn corners. But there was a girl in the class who was better than any of us, and she was an inspiration. It didn't seem to be a hindrance to her that she was blind.

After high school, I bought a sewing machine of my own, and on weekends I took a sewing class. Because sewing required tremendous concentration, it took my mind off everything else in the world. Eventually I made dresses for myself, a bathrobe, and even curtains for my first apartment.

But the stakes were so much higher now. I wanted Laura's dress to be perfect. The pattern was simple—sleeveless with a rounded neck, a full skirt, and a narrow self-belt. After I finished it, I'd decorate it with the roses. I started early in the morning, just after breakfast, and worked through the day with no breaks. When I finished, shortly after dark, I put it up on a hanger and hung it in front of the window. Every time the breeze blew, the dress seemed to sway, as if it were dancing. I sat in front of it, watching how it moved, remembering Laura and feeling the sting of all the could-have-, should-have-beens in her short life. Finally I packed it up into a big box and carefully covered it with tissue paper. I wrapped it with pale pink dotted paper and lavender ribbon. I wrote a card to Laura's mom and brought it to the West Side building where the family lived.

"This is for Laura Morgan's mother," I told the doorman, handing him the box. He looked at me for a long minute.

"We prayed for her," he said, finally. "Every one of us." He shook his head in despair. I looked back at him and nodded. Then I ran outside into the night, forgetting where I was going.

chapter thirty-two

I was feeling down, so I called Arnie to see if he wanted to have dinner. But Arnie wasn't acting like the Arnie I knew. We were finishing a bento box filled with California rolls, vegetable tempura, and teriyaki salmon, from a great new Japanese restaurant where we now got takeout instead of the greasy Chinese place called Hunan Balcony that we rechristened the Human Balcony. But instead of his crooked grin, Arnie just looked glum. I was sure it had something to do with the end of his relationship with the cheese, but I didn't go there. I pushed the last California roll toward him, but he refused it.

"What news from Claude Monet?"

"I wouldn't know." I looked at my watch. "But now, I'm guessing that he's probably in bed with his agent. Otherwise, he's sitting in the garden in the moonlight, drawing inspiration from the landscape."

Vétheuil, with the Seine flowing through it, was supposed to be a spectacular part of France. How did I know? Google University. Monet did a number of paintings there, it said, including several after the frozen river cracked apart following the winter of 1879 and huge blocks of ice rushed down, sweeping up everything in their path. It was said that the thundering noise drew Monet outside to watch.

I also looked at paintings Monet did when he lived there. He was unknown at the time, and so poor he had to live with another family. The turning point for him was a one-man show held at a gallery in the office of the magazine *La Vie Moderne*. Part of his story echoed Luke's—poor artist, just starting out, finally a show that launched him. Even though I was angry with him, I empathized with Luke's interest in staying at a place that reverberated with the history of the great painter.

"I'm sorry, Sage," Arnie said, bringing me back to earth. "Don't you just wish sometimes that things could go easier for you?"

"A lot of people have it much worse," I said, feeling like his schoolteacher. "I don't sit up nights feeling sorry for myself, if that's what you mean." I pushed the bento box further away. He stared at me for a long time, playing with his chopsticks as if they were drum sticks.

"Sage…" he started, and then looked away. "Can I tell you something?"

I looked at him, uncertainly. "Sure, what?"

"You won't laugh?"

"I won't laugh." Anyway, I was out of practice.

"You swear?"

"Arnie, are we ten years old? I swear."

"Okay, here goes." He looked off into the distance, and then back at me. "You know what my real problem is?"

"No," I answered cautiously. *I don't want to hear that he's gay. And please, please no dreaded disease. I can't take any more awful news.* "What, Arnie?"

He exhaled for effect, as if he were about to make a major confession. "Sage, I...I've—I've never been with a woman."

I pushed out my chair and turned to him. "Arnie," I said, almost on the verge of laughing with relief, but choking it back because I knew he'd think I was laughing *at* him. "That's not a terrible thing." I smiled. "I thought that you were going to tell me you had some terrible affliction or something. I'm so relieved."

"No," he said, somberly, "it's not an affliction, but the longer you wait, the worse it gets."

"You'll find someone—you will." I reached for his hand across the table and squeezed it.

"Thanks, Sage." He looked into my eyes. "Thanks for listening."

By the time the weekend was over, Arnie turned into my project. I didn't go to the park with Harry for half the day the way I usually do on Saturdays; I went for an hour, and then took Arnie to my gym to sign him up. Clothes only went so far.

"If you're in great shape, it boosts your ego and your confidence," I told him, like a motivational video. "And when you're in a positive state of mind, things work out better for you."

He looked at me, unsure, and then nodded. "Okay—I'll give it a whirl."

"Work out three or four nights a week. If your body is tight, clothes look better."

"Sage, do you always, like, uh, take over people's lives?"

"That's what they pay me for."

He nodded miserably. "What else?"

After a haircut, we shot over to Bloomingdale's. His fairy godmother was trying to revamp not only his body and wardrobe but also his life. After we shopped, we dropped— all our bundles. We ate scrambled eggs in my apartment and then went to a downtown bar so we could work on his technique.

I was never one to hang out at singles bars. The ridiculous come-on lines nauseated me. But what better way to get Arnie talking to women than to go with him so that he didn't have to walk in alone? We started at W in Union Square, where a drink cost as much as a hot meal, and the crowd was downtown hip. I spotted a cute blonde in a DK suit.

"Tell her she looks great in Donna Karan," I whispered in his ear, above the din.

"What do I say if she asks me how I know it's Donna Karan?"

"Tell her you didn't know for sure, but that she reminded you of the models you see in the Donna Karan ads."

"Sage, maybe you should be writing HBO scripts instead of doing wardrobe counseling."

I scratched the back of my neck. "I never thought of that…and that's a good line too, so now get out of here, and see what happens."

He made a sour face. "Christ, I feel like your puppet."

I turned him around and pushed him away. I studied his body language for a few minutes and then got lost viewing the action around me. Girls were out in pairs, but so were guys. I tried to remember the last time I was at a bar alone and I drew a blank. It made dating sites look appealing. You were judged by your words at first, nothing else.

I finished my wine. Should I order another? Was Arnie coming back? He was still talking to Miss DK at the end of the bar. Instead of going over, I called his cell.

"I'm going to take off. Are you okay to stay?"

"Yeah, fine, I can make lunch tomorrow," he answered, in code.

"Call me later and give me a report."

I went out to Park Avenue and waited for a bus. It was an overcast night. The sky was dark except for a sliver of moonlight. I wondered whether Luke could see the stars, wherever he was.

chapter thirty-three

It was really one of the more bizarre stories of my career. Through another client who referred him, I got a call from a man whose wife had been murdered. He moved to New York from New Jersey, lost a tremendous amount of weight, and he wanted me to buy him new clothes.

Steven Saunders was about forty-five years old. He was an executive with a recruiting firm in New York, and one day while he was at work someone broke into his home in Short Hills, New Jersey. In the middle of the afternoon, his wife walked in on the robbers. The police suspected that when she cried out in surprise, she startled them and they shot her.

Steven was home for two months, so traumatized by the murder that he was unable to function. While he was plump before, afterward he became as gaunt as a long-distance runner. Part of his recommended therapy to fight depression, in fact, was exercise. In addition to his indifference to food and his drastic cut in calories, he started running.

We started out talking about how he felt about himself.

You wouldn't imagine that a man who had gone through a trauma like that would seek out sartorial counseling, but one of his friends suggested he see me, as well as a psychologist and a nutritionist, as part of his support team. After spending a seven-hour day together, most of it talking about everything except clothes, I went home feeling wrung out. My head was ringing with our conversation about his wife, Jean, all his memories of her, and the things he took for granted before that he now realized made their relationship so special.

We didn't talk about clothes until the end of the day. He didn't know what size he was before or after he lost all the weight. He didn't have a tailor. And he had no idea what he wanted me to buy for him. "Jean bought all my clothes," he said. "She hung them up in the closet and I wore them."

I took his measurements and told him I'd shop without him and have it all shipped to his home. There was no way this man could be dragged to the stores and told to try things on.

It was one of the most emotionally wrenching experiences I'd ever had with a client. I ached to come up with things to say that would boost him up, but what? So instead of spouting platitudes, I listened and my heart went out to him. Odd as it was, I thought of Harry. One day he had a family, a home, and a life, and the next day it was all gone and he was alone.

I waved hello to the doorman, dropped the mail, and fed Harry. After eating, he sat with me in front of the television, burrowing into the pillows as though he were trying to carve out a comfortable spot for himself. Sometimes Harry was like an animated stuffed animal, my living security blanket. We curled up together and no matter what else had happened that day, it was okay because we were together.

I channel-surfed until I got to a National Geographic show about a dog that rescued someone from drowning. It was 1995 and a dog named Boo and his owner were walking along the Yuba River in northern California. After they made their way around a bend, the ten-month-old Newfoundland looked out at the water and saw that something was wrong. He tore off into the river, swimming out toward a man who was clinging onto a red gas can, desperate to stay afloat in the powerful current. Boo grabbed the man's arm and towed him back to safety. The man he saved was a deaf-mute, unable to call out for help. The man had fallen into the river when he was gold-dredging.

"Boo had no formal training in water rescue," said Anderson, a Newfoundland breeder for thirty years. "It was just instinct. He picked up on the fact that there was someone in distress and then dealt with the situation." A year later, the Newfoundland Club of America, in Cheyenne, Wyoming, awarded Boo a medal for his heroism.

"Oh Harry," I hugged him as salty tears streamed down my face. I got up to get a treat for him. While he had nothing to do with the rescue, and there was no logic to it at all, I simply wanted to reward him because he was a fellow dog. He ate the biscuit hungrily and waited for another. I hesitated and then handed him a second one.

While I was putting away the bag of banana-apple treats, I noticed the stack of letters by the door. I went over to the pile of mail, and saw just the corner of an envelope. It was pale blue. I pulled it from the stack and saw the violet ink. As my heart amped up, I went into the kitchen for a knife and carefully slit open the envelope.

Dear Sage,

I'm sitting outside of my house looking out at a garden that's planted with a ferocious harmony of red poppies, acid-yellow wildflowers, Spanish lavender, and bushes and boughs of silvery green. I have a dozen or more paints near me and a six-foot canvas, but there's nothing on it.

I thought at first it was just too beautiful here to work—too perfectly art directed by nature, maybe. So I drove further out in the country, to search for a different landscape to inspire me. Something wilder, less harmonious.

But that isn't it. I'm consumed with thinking about you. My focus isn't on what's around me, it's on everything inside my head from missing you. So I got drunk and then I tried to paint. I tried painting sober. I tried to use the canvas as a place to put my fears, my confusion, and my pain, but it didn't work.

You're probably thinking now that we barely know each other. But I feel that on some deeper, visceral level, there's a bond between us—something, actually, that I looked for while I was sketching you—something that I hoped to bring to life on a canvas…if you'd let me. It would have been easier for me to show you.

This is so hard for me to write. I wanted to come here and work. I wanted to be totally on my own. I didn't want to be thinking of you, consumed by you. And in truth, I'd thought that if I left you'd be better off anyway, without me. But things turned out so differently than I expected, and I'm powerless to change what's inside my head now.

It went on for another page. Why was it that Luke poured out his heart only in print? Was he using his writing skills to show what a tortured genius he was—as if that were an excuse for the way he acted? I read the letter again and realized that he literally had a crippling fear of opening himself up in person. It was safe to write. There was a distance. I wanted to call Jennelle, or maybe Mary Alice. Somebody, just to talk to. But what would I say?

My eyes scanned the letter again. There was an address at the bottom, but no phone. What was I supposed to do, write back and wait a month for a response? I felt like Abigail Adams in 1776. There was no way to reach her beloved John in Europe except by writing a letter that would take months to get to him. I put Luke's letter aside and got into bed thinking that this was my first long-distance love affair.

chapter thirty-four

I lost count of the money I had Brian Schulberg spend on his honeymoon. He and Brenda were going to his house in Mustique, the chic island refuge of Mick Jagger and Princess Margaret years back. Aside from bathing suits, both of their wardrobes were heavy on silk and linen as well as cotton T-shirts, cargo pants, and shorts.

For someone who was so seemingly oblivious to what he wore before, it was hard to believe that Brian had become so taken with his new, sleeker image. It was as though he saw himself reborn, a different person from the one who had married and divorced before.

"These are part of my new life, my new me," he said to me one day as I met him for another few hours of shopping. "I have you to thank," he said. I waved away the compliment. "I'm serious," he said. "I never thought about what kind of impression I made before. That matters, at least in the beginning."

Clothes helped him play the part, they were his props.

There was that word again. While Brenda didn't seem terribly preoccupied with what she wore, she loved the idea that I was picking everything out for her and that it would all come out right.

I got home from work and called Arnie. He wasn't home. He was dating the girl he met at W, whom I now dubbed Donna K. I didn't know whether they had a future together, but I knew one thing. After they went out for the second time, he stayed over at her apartment. He didn't discuss the evening. He didn't say a word. But when I left for work the following morning, I ran into him coming in as I was going out. He had on the same suit as the night before. There was no mistaking the crooked grin he gave me as we passed each other in the lobby.

chapter thirty-five

The wonderful thing about living in Manhattan is that food is everywhere and all of it can be delivered to your door. This time I called the local deli and ordered a turkey sandwich. A few minutes later the phone rang. Faster than usual, I thought. Then I looked at the number. It wasn't the deli.

"Sage?"

"Yes," I said, finally.

"It's Luke."

"I know." I didn't know what else to say.

"Did you get my letter?"

"Uh-huh." It sounded as though my voice was going to break. "It was so good to hear from you—after only two months."

I heard him breathe. "Please, I want to see you."

"Where are you?" I asked, cautiously.

"On the phone."

I smirked. "In *France* on the phone?"

"Not anymore."

"Long Island?" I tried to pin him down.

"Outside—your apartment."

I walked to the window and pulled up the shade. He was standing on the corner, leaning up against a car, looking up at the building. "You're crazy."

"I know."

He hung up, and I looked at myself in the mirror. How much can you change your appearance in one hundred and twenty seconds? I ran into the bathroom, grabbed a hairbrush and ran it through my hair, brushed my teeth, fixed my eyeliner, and then circled the apartment like a dizzy dog straightening up. When the doorman rang, my heart pounded so hard it felt like my chest was being caned.

I stood next to the door listening for footsteps. When there was a soft knock, I quietly stepped back so that he wouldn't know I'd been standing on the other side of it. Harry started to bark insanely, the way he always does when someone's in the hall. A moment later, I opened the door.

He had that signature half smile on his face, his eyes studying me to see if my face looked the way he remembered. He looked shy, vulnerable. He was wearing jeans and the brown leather bomber jacket with a black T-shirt underneath.

"I shouldn't let you in," I said, flatly, eventually stepping aside so he could walk in. "How could you just show up?" I leaned against the back of the couch and glared at him. "You disappear for two months and then you call from downstairs?"

"Don't be mad."

"You never said you were going, you never called." I closed my eyes. "I don't understand you."

"I couldn't face telling you I was leaving," he said, taking a step toward me and then running a hand through his hair. "I didn't know when I rented the place that I would get involved with you, that I would feel this way." He walked toward me and put his arms around me, burying his face in the side of my hair.

"I thought if I just went away it would be easier for both of us," he whispered. "You'd be better off without me. I'd be working in new surroundings. I thought it would give my work a new energy…but it didn't work out that way."

A moment later, the doorman rang again and I jumped. I struggled to break free.

"Wait." I picked up the intercom. "Food delivery," the doorman said.

"You're just in time for my turkey sandwich."

"Good," he said. "I'm starved."

Luke's bedroom in Vétheuil was a bare room that he painted sky blue, he said. There was a double bed and an armoire. Nothing else. It faced floor-to-ceiling French doors that opened out to the garden with a view of the river. When he woke in the morning, it was the first thing he saw. We were lying in my bed, which faced a triple-size window that looked out at apartment buildings. There were no flowers, unless you counted the pot of geraniums on the terrace of the building across Third Avenue that faced mine. There were a few trees on the street, but they were young and didn't reach beyond the second floor.

"You take vacations," he said. "So take one now. Come back with me for two or three weeks, and a month later, I'll come back, for good."

I thought about all the clients whose closets I had promised to do, and all the people whose images I hoped to improve. My calendar was filled for the next month. Then I thought about my own life, and how I needed to improve it. "I'd have to call and change a million appointments."

"So?"

I started toying with the small gold earring in his left ear. I leaned over him and kissed the side of his neck. He moaned with pleasure and pulled me against his chest. It was smooth and warm. I pressed my cheek against it and listened to his heart.

I started thinking about my client whose wife was murdered and how haunted he was by all the things they'd never get a chance to do together. I thought about Laura and all the life ahead of her that she never had a chance to live and all the boys she might have met and dated and loved, but now never would. And I thought about Mary Alice and the house she hoped to build for her mother, but never had a chance to.

"You can't waste time agonizing about life; you have to go after what you want, Sage," she'd said. "It all can change in a minute."

I reached out and ran my fingers along the side of his face. "I'll go," I said, kissing him, not able to stop. "I will."